B.L Farjeon

The Shield of Love

B.L Farjeon

The Shield of Love

1st Edition | ISBN: 978-3-75235-033-3

Place of Publication: Frankfurt am Main, Germany

Year of Publication: 2020

Outlook Verlag GmbH, Germany.

THE SHIELD OF LOVE

BY

B. L. FARJEON

CHAPTER I.

This is not exactly a story of Cinderella, although a modern Cinderella—of whom there are a great many more in our social life than people wot of— plays her modest part therein; and the allusion to one of the world's prettiest fairy-tales is apposite enough because her Prince, an ordinary English gentleman prosaically named John Dixon, was first drawn to her by the pity which stirs every honest heart when innocence and helplessness are imposed upon. Pity became presently sweetened by affection, and subsequently glorified by love, which, at the opening of our story, awaited its little plot of fresh-smelling earth to put forth its leaves, the healthy flourishing of which has raised to the dignity of a heavenly poem that most beautiful of all words, Home.

Her Christian name was Charlotte, her surname Fox-Cordery, and she had a mother and a brother. These, from the time her likeness to Cinderella commenced, comprised the household.

Had it occurred to a stranger who gazed for the first time upon Mr. and Miss Fox-Cordery, as they sat in the living-room of the Fox-Cordery establishment, that for some private reason the brother and sister had dressed in each other's clothes, he might well have been excused the fancy. It was not that the lady was so much like a gentleman, but that the gentleman was so much like a lady; and a closer inspection would certainly have caused the stranger to do justice at least to Miss Fox-Cordery. She was the taller and stouter of the twain, and yet not too tall or stout for grace and beauty of an attractive kind. There was some color in her face, his was perfectly pallid, bearing the peculiar hue observable in waxwork figures; her eyes were black, his blue; her hair was brown, his sandy; and the waxwork suggestion was strengthened by his whiskers and mustache, which had a ludicrous air of having been stuck on. There was a cheerful energy in her movements which was conspicuously absent in his, and her voice had a musical ring in it, while his was languid and deliberate. She was his junior by a good ten years, her age being twenty-eight, but had he proclaimed himself no more than thirty,

2

only those who were better informed would have disputed the statement. When men and women reach middle age the desire to appear younger than they are is a pardonable weakness, and it was to the advantage of Mr. Fox-Cordery that it was less difficult for him than for most of us to maintain the harmless fiction.

This was not the only bubble which Mr. Fox-Cordery was ready to encourage in order to deceive the world. His infantile face, his appealing blue eyes, his smooth voice, were traps which brought many unwary persons to grief. Nature plays numberless astonishing tricks, but few more astonishing than that which rendered the contrast between the outer and inner Mr. Fox-Cordery even more startling than that which existed in the physical characteristics of this brother and sister.

There were other contrasts which it may be as well to mention. As brother and sister they were of equal social rank, but the equality was not exhibited in their attire. Mr. Fox-Cordery would have been judged to be a man of wealth, rich enough to afford himself all the luxuries of life; Charlotte would have been judged a young woman who had to struggle hard for a living, which, indeed, was not far from the truth, for she was made to earn her bread and butter, if ever woman was. Her clothing was common and coarse, and barely sufficient, the length of her frock being more suitable to a girl of fifteen than to a woman of twenty-eight. This was not altogether a drawback, for Charlotte had shapely feet and ankles, but they would have been seen to better advantage in neat boots or shoes than in the worn-out, down-at-heels slippers she wore. Depend upon it she did not wear them from choice, for every right-minded woman takes a proper pride in her boots and shoes, and in her stockings, gloves, and hats. The slippers worn at the present moment by Charlotte were the only available coverings for her feet she had. True, there was a pair of boots in the house which would fit no other feet than hers, but they were locked up in her mother's wardrobe. Then her stockings. Those she had on were of an exceedingly rusty black, and had been darned and darned till scarcely a vestige of their original self remained. Another and a better pair she ought to have had the right to call her own, and these were in the house, keeping company with her boots. In her poorly furnished bedroom you would have searched in vain for hat or gloves; these were likewise under lock and key, with a decent frock and mantle she was allowed to wear on special occasions, at the will of her taskmasters. So that she was considerably worse off in these respects than many a poor woman who lives with her husband and children in a garret.

But for all this Charlotte was a pleasant picture to gaze upon, albeit just now her features wore rather a grave expression. She had not an ornament on her person, not a brooch or a ring, but her hair was luxuriant and abundant, and was carefully brushed and coiled; her neck was white, and her figure graceful; and though in a couple of years she would be in her thirties, there was a youthfulness in her appearance which can only be accounted for by her fortunate inheritance of a cheerful spirit, of which, drudge as she was, her mother and her brother could not rob her.

This precious inheritance she derived from her father, who had transmitted to her all that was spiritually best in his nature: and nothing else. It was not because he did not love his daughter that she was left unendowed, but because of a fatal delay in the disposition of his world's goods. Procrastination may be likened to an air-gun carrying a deadly bullet. Mr. Fox-Cordery, the younger, "took" after his mother. Occasionally in life these discrepant characteristics are found grouped together in one family, the founders of which, by some strange chance, have become united, instead of flying from each other, as do certain violently antagonistic chemicals when an attempt is made to unite them in a friendly partnership. The human repulsion occurs afterward, when it is too late to repair the evil. If marriages are made in heaven, as some foolish people are in the habit of asserting, heaven owes poor mortality a debt it can never repay.

Far different from Charlotte's was Mr. Fox-Cordery's appearance. As to attire it was resplendent and magnificent, if these terms may be applied to a mortal of such small proportions. He was excruciatingly careful in the combing and brushing of his hair, but in the effect produced he could not reach her point of excellence, and this drawback he inwardly construed into a wrong inflicted upon him by her. He often struck a mental balance after this fashion, and brought unsuspecting persons in his debt. Moreover, he would have liked to change skins with her, and give her his waxy hue for her pearly whiteness. Could the exchange have been effected by force he would have had it done. At an early stage of manhood he had been at great pains to impart an upward curly twist to his little mustache, in the hope of acquiring a military air, but the attempt was not successful, and his barber, after long travail, had given it up in despair, and had advised him to train his mustache in the way it was inclined to go.

"Let it droop, sir," said the barber, "it will look beautiful so. There's a sentiment in a drooping mustache that always attracts the sex."

The argument was irresistible, and Mr. Fox-Cordery's little mustache was allowed to droop and to grow long; and it certainly did impart to his countenance a dreaminess of expression which its wearer regarded as a partial compensation for the disappointment of his young ambition. No man in the world ever bestowed more attention upon his person, or took greater pains to make himself pleasing in the sight of his fellow-creatures, than did Mr. Fox-Cordery; and this labor of love was undertaken partly from vanity, partly from cunning. A good appearance deceived the world; it put people off their guard; if you wished to gain a point it was half the battle. He spent hours every week with his tailor, the best in London, discussing fits and fashions, trying on coats, vests, and trousers, ripping and unripping to conquer a crease, and suggesting a little more padding here, and a trifle less there. His hats and boots were marvels of polish, his shirts and handkerchiefs of the finest texture, his neckties marvels, his silk socks and underwear dainty and elegant, and his pins and, rings would have passed muster with the most censorious of fashion's votaries. He was spick and span from the crown of his head to the soles of his feet. As he walked along the streets, picking his way carefully, or sat in his chair with his small legs crossed, he was a perfect little model of a man, in animated pallid waxwork. He preferred to sit instead of stand; being long-waisted it gave beholders a false impression of his height.

From his cradle he had been his mother's idol and his father's terror. Mrs. Fox-Cordery ruled the roost, and her husband, preferring peace to constant warfare, gave the reins into her hands, and allowed her to do exactly as she pleased. This meant doing everything that would give pleasure to the Fox-Cordery heir, who soon discovered his power and made use of it to his own advantage. What a tyrant in the domestic circle was the little mannikin! The choicest tidbits at meals, the food he liked best, the coolest place in summer, and warmest in winter, all were conceded to him. He tortured birds and cats openly, and pinched servants on the sly. The good-tempered, cheerful-hearted father used to gaze in wonder at his son, and speculate ruefully upon the kind of man he was likely to grow into.

When young Fox-Cordery was near his eleventh birthday Charlotte was born, and as the mother held the son to her heart, so did the father hold the daughter to his. They became comrades, father and daughter on one side, mother and son on the other, with no sympathies in common. Mr. Fox-Cordery took his little daughter for long rides and walks, told her fairy stories, and gave her country feasts; and it is hard to say who enjoyed them most.

The introduction of Charlotte into young Fox-Cordery's life afforded him new sources of delight. He pinched her on the sly as he pinched the servants, he pulled her ears, he slapped her face, and the wonder of it was that Charlotte never complained. Her patience and submission did not soften him; he tyrannized over her the more. Hearing his father say that Charlotte ought to have a doll, he said that he would buy her one, and the father was pleased at this prompting of affection. Obtaining a sum of money from his mother, young Fox-Cordery put half of it into his pocket, and expended the other half in the purchase of a doll with a woebegone visage, dressed in deep mourning. Presenting it to his sister he explained that the doll had lost everybody belonging to her, and was the most wretched and miserable doll in existence.

"She will die soon," he said, "and then I will give you a coffin."

But the young villain's purpose was foiled by Charlotte's sweet disposition. The poor doll, being alone in the world, needed sympathy and consolation, and Charlotte wept over her, and kissed and fondled her, and did everything in her power to make her forget her sorrows. Eventually Charlotte's father suggested that the doll had been in mourning long enough and he had her dressed like a bride, and restored to joy and society; but this so enraged young Fox-Cordery that he got up in the night and tore the bridal dress to shreds, and chopped the doll into little pieces.

The fond companionship between Mr. Fox-Cordery and his daughter did not last very long. Before Charlotte was seven years old her father died. On his deathbed the thought occurred to him that his daughter was unprovided for.

His will, made shortly after his marriage, when he was still in ignorance of his wife's true character, left everything unreservedly to her; and now, when he was passing into the valley of the Shadow of Death, he trembled for his darling Charlotte's future. The illness by which he was stricken down had been sudden and unexpected, and he had not troubled to alter his will, being confident that many years of life were before him. And now there was little time left. But he lived still; he could repair the error; he yet could make provision for his little girl. Lying helpless, almost speechless, on his bed, he motioned to his wife, and made her understand that he wished to see his lawyer. She understood more; she divined his purpose. She had read the will, by which she would become the sole inheritor of his fortune—she and her son, for all she had would be his. Should she allow her beloved Fox to be robbed, and should she assist in despoiling him? Her mind was quickly made up.

"I will send for the lawyer," she said to her husband.

"At once, at once!"

"Yes, at once."

A day passed.

"Has the lawyer come?" whispered the dying man to his wife.

"He was in the country when I wrote yesterday," she replied. "He returns to-morrow morning, and will be here then."

"There must be no delay," said he.

His wife nodded, and bade him be easy in his mind.

"Excitement is bad for you," she said. "The lawyer is sure to come."

He knew that it would be dangerous for him to agitate himself, and he fell asleep, holding the hand of his darling child. In the night he awoke, and prayed for a few days of life, and that his senses would not forsake him before the end came. His wife, awake in the adjoining room, prayed also, but it will be charitable to draw a veil over her during those silent hours.

Another day passed, and again he asked for his lawyer.

"He called," said his wife, "but you were asleep, and I would not have you disturbed."

It was false; she had not written to the lawyer.

That night the dying man knew that his minutes were numbered, and that he would not see another sunrise in this world. Speech had deserted him; he was helpless, powerless. He looked piteously at his wife, who would not admit any person into the room but herself, with the exception of her children and the doctor. She answered his look with a smile, and with false tenderness smoothed his pillow. The following morning the doctor called again, and as he stood by the patient's bedside observed him making some feeble signs which he could not understand. Appealing to Mrs. Fox-Cordery, she interpreted the signs to him.

"He wishes to know the worse," she said.

The doctor beckoned her out of the room, and told her she must prepare for it.

"Soon?" she inquired, with her handkerchief to her dry eyes.

"Before midnight," he said gravely, and left her to her grief.

She did not deprive her husband of his last sad comfort; she brought their daughter to him, and placed her by his side. Mrs. Fox-Cordery remained in the room, watching the clock. "Before midnight, before midnight," she whispered to herself a score of times.

The prince of the house, soon to be king, came to wish his father farewell. There was not speck or spot upon the young man, who had been from home all day, and had just returned. During this fatal illness he had been very little with his father.

"What is the use of my sitting mum chance by his bedside?" he said to his mother. "I can't do him any good; and I don't think he cares for me much. All he thinks of is that brat."

Charlotte was the brat, and she gazed with large solemn eyes upon her brother as he now entered the chamber of death. He was dressed in the height of fashion, and he did not remove his gloves as he pressed his father's clammy hand, and brushed with careless lips the forehead upon which the dews of death were gathering. Then he wiped his mouth with his perfumed handkerchief, and longed to get out of the room to smoke. The father turned his dim eyes upon the fashionably attired young man, standing there so neat and trim and fresh, as if newly turned out of a bandbox, and from him to Charlotte in an old cotton dress, her hair in disorder, and her face stained with tears. Maybe a premonition of his little girl's future darkened his last moments, but he was too feeble to express it. Needless to dwell upon the scene, pregnant and suggestive as it was. The doctor's prediction was verified; when the bells tolled the midnight hour Mr. Fox-Cordery had gone to his rest, and Charlotte was friendless in her mother's house.

CHAPTER II.

Poor Cinderella.

Then commenced a new life for the girl; she became a drudge, and was made to do servants' work, and to feel that there was no love for her beneath the roof that sheltered her. She accepted the position unmurmuringly, and slaved and toiled with a willing spirit. Early in the morning, while her tyrants were snug abed, she was up and doing, and though she never succeeded in pleasing them and was conscious that she had done her best, she bore their scolding and fault-finding without a word of remonstrance. They gave her no schooling, and yet she learned to read and write, and to speak good English. There were hidden forces in the girl which caused her to supply, by unwearying industry, the deficiencies of her education. Hard as was her life she had compensations, which sprang from the sweetness of her nature.

Her early acquaintance with errand boys and tradesmen's apprentices led her into the path strewn with lowly flowers. She became familiar with the struggles of the poor, and, sympathizing with them, she performed many acts of kindness which brought happiness to her young heart; and though from

8

those who should have shown her affection she received constant rebuffs, she was not soured by them.

The treatment she and her brother met with in the home in which they each had an equal right, and should have had an equal share, was of a painfully distinctive character. Nothing was good enough for him; anything was good enough for her. Very well; she ministered to him without repining. He and his mother took their pleasures together, and Charlotte was never invited to join them, and never asked to be invited. There was no interchange of confidences between them. They had secrets which they kept from her; she had secrets which she kept from them. Those shared by Mr. Fox-Cordery and his mother savored of meanness and trickery; Charlotte's were sweet and charitable. They did not open their hearts to her because of the fear that she might rebel against the injustice which was being inflicted upon her; she did not open her heart to them because she felt that they would not sympathize with her. They would have turned up their noses at the poor flowers she cherished, and would have striven to pluck them from her—and, indeed, the attempt was made, fortunately without success.

Charlotte's practical acquaintance with kitchen work, and the economical spirit in which she was enjoined by her mother to carry out her duties, taught her the value of scraps of food, a proper understanding of which would do a great many worthy people no harm. Recognizing that the smallest morsels could be turned to good account, she allowed nothing to be thrown away or wasted. Even the crumbs would furnish meals for birds, and they were garnered with affectionate care. She was well repaid in winter and early spring for her kindness to the feathered creatures, some of which she believed really grew to know her, and it is a fact that none were frightened of her. Many pretty little episodes grew out of this association which was the cause of genuine pleasure to Charlotte, and she discovered in these lowly ways of life treasures which such lofty people as her mother and brother never dreamed of. If she had authority nowhere else in her home she had some in the kitchen, so every scrap of food was looked after, collected, and given to pensioners who were truly grateful for them. These pensioners were all small children, waifs of the gutters, of whom there are shoals in every great city. Thus it will be seen that the position assigned to Charlotte by her mother and brother ennobled and enriched her spiritually; it brought into play her best and sweetest qualities.

Her charities were dispensed with forethought and wisdom, and Mr. Fox-Cordery took no greater pains in the adornment of his person than Charlotte did to make her scraps of food palatable to the stomachs of her little pensioners. With half an onion, nicely shredded, and the end of a stray carrot, she produced of these scraps a stew which did her infinite credit as a cook of odds and ends; and it was a sight worth seeing to watch her preparing such a savory meal for the bare-footed youngsters who came at nightfall to the kitchen entrance of her home.

When these proceedings were discovered by her mother she was ordered to discontinue them, but in this one instance she showed a spirit of rebellion, and maintained her right to give away the leavings instead of throwing them into the dustbin. That she was allowed to have her way was perhaps the only concession made to her in her servitude.

For an offense of another kind, however, she was made to pay dearly.

She obtained permission one evening to go out for a walk, an hour to the minute being allowed her. On these occasions, which were rare, she always chose the poorer thoroughfares for her rambles, and as she now strolled through a narrow street she came upon a woman, with a baby in her arms, sitting on a doorstep. Pity for the wan face, of which she caught just one glance, caused Charlotte to stop and speak to the woman. The poor creature was in the last stage of want and destitution, and Charlotte's heart bled as she listened to the tale of woe. The wail of the hungry babe sent a shiver through the sympathizing girl. She could not bear to leave the sufferers, and yet what good could be done by remaining? She had not a penny to give them. Charlotte never had any money of her own, it being part of the system by which her life was ruled to keep her absolutely penniless. She learned from the poor woman that every article of clothing she possessed that could with decency be dispensed with had found its way to the pawn-shop.

"See," said the wretched creature, raising her ragged frock.

It was all there was on her body.

The pitiful revelation inspired Charlotte. She had on a flannel and a cotton petticoat. Stepping aside into the shadow of an open door she loosened the strings of her petticoats, and they slipped to the ground.

"Take these," said the young girl, and ran home as fast as she could.

She was a few minutes behind her time, and her mother was on the watch for her. Upon Charlotte making her appearance she was informed that she would never be allowed out again, and she stood quietly by without uttering a word of expostulation. The scene ended by Charlotte being ordered instantly to bed, and to secure obedience Mrs. Fox-Cordery accompanied her daughter to her bedroom. There, on undressing, the loss of the two petticoats was discovered. Mrs. Fox-Cordery demanded an explanation and it was given to her, and the result was that every article of Charlotte's clothing was taken from her room, and locked in her mother's wardrobe. There was not so much as a lace or a piece of tape left. But, stripped as she was of every possession, Charlotte, as she lay in the darkness and silence of her dark room, was not sorry for her charitable deed. She thought of the poor woman and her babe, and was glad that they had something to eat; and she was sure, if the same thing occurred again, that she would act as she had already done.

The next morning early, Mrs. Fox-Cordery unlocked the door of her daughter's bedroom, and entered with a bundle of clothes in her arms. Though it was imperative that Charlotte should be punished for her bad behavior, there was work in the kitchen to do, and the girl was not to be allowed to dawdle all day in bed because she had misconducted herself. That would be a reward, not a punishment.

"Your brother and I have been talking about you," said Mrs. Fox-Cordery. "He is shocked at your behavior. If you have the least sense of what is right you will beg him to forgive you."

"Why should I do that?" asked Charlotte, pondering a little upon the problem presented to her. "I have not hurt him in any way."

"Did you not hear me say," exclaimed Mrs. Fox-Cordery, frowning, "that he is shocked at your behavior? Is that not hurting him?"

"Not that I can see, mother," replied Charlotte. "I cannot help it if he looks upon what I have done in a wrong light."

"In a wrong light, Miss Impertinence!" cried Mrs. Fox-Cordery. "The view your brother takes of a thing is always right."

"If you will give me my clothes," said Charlotte, with pardonable evasion, "I will get up."

"You will get up when I order you, and not before. I am speaking to you by your brother's instructions, and we will have this matter out, once and for all."

Charlotte lay silent. It did not appear to her that she had anything to defend, and she instinctively felt that the most prudent course was to say as little as possible.

"Will you tell your brother that you are sorry for what you have done, or shall I?"

"I am not sorry, mother."

Mrs. Fox-Cordery was rather staggered by this reply.

"There is an absence of moral perception in you," she said severely, "that will lead to bad results. If you were not my daughter I should call in a policeman."

Charlotte opened her eyes wide, and she shivered slightly. She was neither a theorist nor a logician; she never debated with herself whether a contemplated action was right or wrong; she simply did what her nature guided her to do. A policeman in her eyes was a blue-frocked, helmeted creature who held unknown terrors in his hand, which he meted out to those who had been guilty of some dreadful action. Of what dreadful action had she been guilty that her mother should drag a policeman into the conversation? It was this reflection that caused her to shiver.

"You gave away last night," said Mrs. Fox-Cordery, regarding the symptom of fear with satisfaction, "what did not belong to you."

"My clothes are my own," pleaded Charlotte.

"They are not your own. They represent property, and every description of property in this family belongs to me and to your brother. The clothes you wear are lent to you for the time being, and by disposing of them as you have done you have committed a theft. You are sharp enough, I presume, to know what a theft is."

"Yes," said Charlotte. Monstrous as was the proposition, she was unable to advance any argument in confutation.

"That we do not punish you as you deserve," pursued Mrs. Fox-Cordery, "is entirely due to your brother's mercy. We will take care that you do not repeat the offense. Such clothes as you are permitted to wear will be given to you as occasion requires; and everything will be marked in my name—you shall do the marking yourself—in proof that nothing belongs to you. Dress yourself now, and go to your work."

"Mother," said Charlotte, getting out of bed, opening her little chest of drawers, and looking round the room, "you have taken everything away from me."

"Yes, everything."

"But something is mine, mother."

"Nothing is yours."

"Father gave me his picture; let me have that back."

"You will have nothing back. We will see how you behave in the future, and you will be treated accordingly. Before you go downstairs pray for a more thankful heart, and for sufficient sense to make you appreciate our goodness. Have you any message to send to your brother?"

"No, mother."

"As I supposed. It is a mystery to me how I ever came to have such a child."

Charlotte said her prayers before she left her bedroom; her father had taught her to do so, night and morning; but she did not pray for a more thankful heart, nor for sense to make her appreciative of the goodness of the family tyrants. Perhaps she was dull; perhaps she failed to discover cause for gratitude; certain it is that she was selfish enough to pray for her father's picture back, a prayer that was never answered. And it is also certain that she had a wonderful power of endurance, which enabled her to bear the heavy burden of domestic tyranny, and even to be happy under it.

From that morning she was practically a prisoner in her home, and the course of her daily life was measured out to her, as it were, from hour to hour. And still she preserved her cheerfulness and sweetness and snatched some gleams of sunshine from her gloomy surroundings.

A brighter gleam shone upon her when, a woman of twenty-five, she made the acquaintance of John Dixon, who for twelve months or so came regularly to the house on business of a confidential nature with Mr. Fox-Cordery. This business connection was broken violently and abruptly, but not before the star of love was shining in Charlotte's heart; and when her lover was turned from the door she bade him good-by with a smile, for she felt that he would be true to her through weal or woe.

CHAPTER III.

A Family Discussion.

Charlotte sat at the window, darning stockings; Mr. Fox-Cordery sat at the table killing flies.

There are more ways than one of killing flies, and there is something to be said about the pastime on the score of taste. The method adopted by Mr. Fox-Cordery was peculiar and original. He had before him a tumbler and a bottle, and he was smoking a cigar. The tumbler was inverted, and into it the operator had inveigled a large number of flies, which he stupefied with smoke. The cigar he was smoking was a particularly fragrant one, and the flies could not therefore complain that they were being shabbily treated. When they were rendered completely helpless he transferred them to the bottle, taking the greatest possible care to keep it corked after each fresh importation, in order that the prisoners should not have the opportunity of escaping in any chance moment of restored animation. By this means Mr. Fox-Cordery had collected some hundreds of flies, whose dazed flutterings and twitchings he watched with languorous interest, his air being that of a man whose thoughts were running upon other matters almost, if not quite, as important as this. He continued at his occupation until the tumbler was empty and the bottle nearly full; and then he threw the stump of his cigar out of window, and, with a smart wrench at the cork, put the bottle on the mantelshelf. He rose, and stood beside his sister.

"Did Mr. Dixon give you no inkling of what he wanted to see me about?" he asked, in his low, languid voice.

"None whatever," replied Charlotte, drawing the stocking she was darning from her left hand, and stretching it this way and that, to assure herself that the work was well done. They were her own stockings she was mending, and Heaven knows how many times they had gone through the process.

"And you did not inquire?"

"I did not inquire."

Some note in her voice struck Mr. Fox-Cordery as new and strange, and he regarded her more attentively.

"The old affair, I suppose," he said maliciously.

"If you mean that Mr. Dixon has any intention of reopening the subject with you," said Charlotte, laying aside the sorely-darned stocking and taking up its fellow, "you are mistaken."

Perhaps the act of stooping had brought the blood to her face, for there was a flush upon it when she lifted her head.

"It is not often that I am."

"Yet it may happen."

The flush in her face had died away, and she was now gravely attending to her work.

Mr. Fox-Cordery pulled down the ends of his little silky mustache. "Be careful how you address me, Charlotte. It is a long time since you and Mr. Dixon met."

14

"No; we have seen each other several times this past year."

"You made no mention to me of these meetings."

"There was no reason why I should, Fox."

"Did you inform mother?"

"That is an unnecessary question. Had I informed her you would not have remained in ignorance. Mother keeps nothing from you."

"You have grown into a particularly intelligent young woman," he said, and added spitefully, "Well, not exactly a young woman—" pausing to note the effect of the shot.

"I am twenty-eight," said Charlotte, in her usual tone, "and you, Fox, will be forty soon."

Her shot told better than his. "We will not continue the conversation," he said shortly.

"As you please, Fox."

He stepped to the fireplace, gave the bottle of flies a violent shake, looked at Charlotte as if he would have liked to serve her the same, and then resumed his place by the window, and drummed upon a pane.

"Mr. Dixon's visit here was a presumption. How dare he intrude himself into this house?"

"Settle it when he calls again," said Charlotte. "He came to see you upon some business or other."

"Which you insist upon concealing from me."

"Indeed I do not. I cannot tell you what I do not know."

"At three o'clock, you say?"

"Yes, at three o'clock."

"I will consider whether he shall be admitted. Don't move, Charlotte."

There was a fly on her hair, which he caught with a lightning sweep of his hand. As he thrust his unfortunate prisoner into the bottle he chuckled at the expression of disgust on Charlotte's face. The fly disposed of, he said:

"Mother shall judge whether you are right or wrong."

"Don't put yourself to unnecessary trouble," said Charlotte. "I can tell you beforehand how she will decide."

The entrance of Mrs. Fox-Cordery did not cause her to raise her head; she proceeded with her darning, and awaited the attack of the combined forces. A singular resemblance existed between mother and son. Her face, like his, was of the hue of pallid wax, her eyes were blue, her hair sandy, and she spoke in a low and languid voice. She held an open letter in her hand.

"Here is a house that will suit you, my love," she said, holding out the letter to him. "It faces the river; there is a nice piece of meadow-land, and a lawn, and a garden with flowers and fruit trees. It stands alone in its own grounds, and there is a little arm of the river you may almost call your own, with a rustic bridge stretching to the opposite bank. The terms are rather high, twelve guineas a week for not less than three months, paid in advance, but I think we must go and see it. I should say it is exactly the place to suit your purpose."

Charlotte listened in wonder. This contemplated removal to a house near the river was new to her—and what scheme was Fox engaged upon that would be furthered by a proceeding so entirely novel? Mr. Fox-Cordery put the letter in his pocket without reading it, and said in a displeased tone:

"We will speak of it by and by."

Mrs. Fox-Cordery glanced sharply from her son to her daughter.

"Charlotte, what have you been doing to annoy Fox?"

"Nothing," replied Charlotte.

"She can prevaricate, you know, mother," observed Mr. Fox-Cordery quietly.

"Of course she can prevaricate. Have we not had innumerable instances of it?"

"I will finish my work in my own room," said Charlotte rising.

"Do not stir," commanded Mrs. Fox-Cordery, "till permission is given you. Fox, my love, what has she done?"

"Mr. Dixon has paid a visit to Charlotte in this house."

"Impossible!"

"Fox has stated what is not correct," said Charlotte, resuming her seat and her work. "Mr. Dixon called to see Fox."

"That is her version," said Mr. Fox-Cordery. "She seeks to excuse herself by throwing it upon me."

"Your conduct is disgraceful," said Mrs. Fox-Cordery to her daughter, "and I am ashamed of you."

"I have done nothing disgraceful," retorted Charlotte, "and I am not ashamed of myself."

Mrs. Fox-Cordery stared at her in astonishment, and Mr. Fox-Cordery nodded his head two or three times, and said:

"You observe a change in Charlotte. There was a time when she would not have dared to put her will in opposition to ours, but I think I shall be found equal to my duty as master of this house. I do not say I am perfect, but I know of what I am capable. I have had my crosses and disappointments; I have had my sorrows. I have them still. Let us, at least, have harmony in our home."

"Amen!" intoned Mrs. Fox-Cordery, with a reproachful look at Charlotte.

"There is but one way," continued Mr. Fox-Cordery, "to secure this harmony. By obedience to orders. I am the head of this house and family, and I will not be thwarted or slighted."

"I will support you, my love," said his mother, "in all ways."

"I never for a moment doubted you, mother. We will not be uncharitable to Charlotte; we will be, as we have ever been, tender and considerate toward her. She inherits a family characteristic which she turns to a wrong account. Tenacity is an excellent quality, but when it is in alliance with intense selfishness, it is productive of great mischief. I am not a hard man; my nature is tender and susceptible, and I am easily led. Convince me that I am wrong in any impression I have formed, and I yield instantly. I learn from Charlotte, mother, that she has been in the habit of meeting Mr. Dixon during the last year in a clandestine and secret manner."

Before Mrs. Fox-Cordery could express her horror at this revelation, Charlotte interposed:

"Fox is misrepresenting me. What I told him was that Mr. Dixon and I have seen each other several times. We have not met secretly or clandestinely."

"You met without our knowledge or sanction," said Mr. Fox-Cordery, "and it comes to the same thing."

"Quite the same thing," assented his mother.

"_I_ never equivocate," said Mr. Fox-Cordery, in his most amiable tone, "_I_ am never evasive. When Mr. Dixon was on friendly terms with us, he was admitted freely into our family circle, and was made welcome. For reasons which I need not enter into I was compelled to sunder all association with him, and to forbid him the house. You, mother, knowing my character, will know whether I was justified or not."

"Who should know you better than your mother?" said Mrs. Fox-Cordery fondly. "I am not acquainted with your reasons, but I am satisfied that they were just. Have you yet to learn, Charlotte, that your brother is the soul of honor and justice?"

Mr. Fox-Cordery waited for Charlotte's indorsement, but she was obstinately silent, and he proceeded:

"It would have been natural, in the attitude I was compelled to assume toward Mr. Dixon, that every member of my family should have had confidence in me, for I was working in their interest. Unfortunately, it was not so; Charlotte stood aloof, probably because I had discovered that a secret understanding existed between her and Mr. Dixon."

"There was none," said Charlotte indignantly. "What was known to Mr. Dixon and myself was known to you and mother. I see no reason to be ashamed of the avowal that we loved each other."

"The avowal is coarse and indelicate," said Mrs. Fox-Cordery, with a frown.

Mr. Fox-Cordery held out his hands, palms upward, as expressing, "What can one expect of a person so wrong-headed as Charlotte?"

"I trust," said Charlotte, with a bright blush on her face, "that the confession of an honest attachment is not a disgrace. You used to speak in the highest terms of Mr. Dixon."

"We live to be deceived," said Mr. Fox-Cordery, sadly surveying the ceiling, "to find our confidence abused. We create an ideal, and discover, too late, that we have been worshiping a mask, the removal of which sends a shudder through our"—he could not find the word he wanted, so he added —"system."

His mother's eyes were fixed admiringly upon him, but there was no admiration in Charlotte's face as, with her hand to her heart, she said boldly:

"You are fond of using fine phrases, Fox, but I do not think you believe in them."

"I am not to be deterred by insults from doing my duty," he replied. "Mr. Dixon asked permission to pay his addresses to you, and, as your natural guardians and protectors, we refused. That should have put an end to the affair."

"I should be justified in asking you," said Charlotte, "whether you think other persons have feelings as well as yourself. If I were to interfere in your love matters I wonder what you would say."

18

"The cases are different," said Mr. Fox-Cordery pathetically. "I am a man; you are a woman."

"Yes," said Charlotte, with bitterness, "I am a woman, and am therefore expected to sacrifice myself. Have you finished, Fox?"

"There is only this to say. It is your mother's command, and mine, that the intimacy between you and Mr. Dixon shall cease. We will not allow it to continue."

He gave his mother a prompting glance.

"Your brother has expressed it correctly," she said. "We will not receive Mr. Dixon into our family. He is an utterly objectionable person, and we will have nothing to do with him. If you have a grain of decent feeling in you, you will obey. Now you can go to your room."

CHAPTER IV.

Wherein Cinderella Asserts Herself.

CHARLOTTE rose, work in hand, and went toward the door, they following her with their eyes, desiring her obedience and approving of it, and yet curious to ascertain what was passing in her mind. For that she was unusually stirred was evident from her manner, which was that of one who had been beaten down all her life, and in whom the seeds of rebellion were struggling to force themselves into light. Suddenly she turned and faced them, and they saw in her eyes the spirit of a brave resolve.

"You have spoken plainly to me," she said. "I must speak plainly to you."

"Go to your room this instant," sternly said her mother.

That the hard cold voice should have given her fresh courage, was a novel experience to them; generally it compelled obedience, but now it had failed. It seemed, indeed, as if she had burst the bonds of oppression which had held her fast for so many years.

"Not till I have said what I have to say, mother. It is something you ought to hear." She paused a moment before she continued. "It is three years ago this very day since we had our last conversation about Mr. Dixon."

"Really!" exclaimed Mrs. Fox-Cordery, and would have expressed herself more violently had not her son restrained her with a warning look, which meant, "Let her go on; she will be sure to commit herself."

"Mr. Dixon was in the habit for some time of coming regularly to the house, and his visits formed the pleasantest remembrances in my life, with the exception of the happy years when my dear father was alive."

"Your dear father, indeed!" was Mrs. Fox-Cordery's scornful comment.

"From the date of my dear father's death," said Charlotte steadily; she was speaking now calmly and resolutely, "Mr. Dixon is the only gentleman who has shown me any consideration, and who has made me feel that I have some claim to a higher position in this house than that of a menial. I am ignorant of the nature of his business with Fox—"

"I will enlighten you," interposed Mr. Fox-Cordery; "he was in my employ, a paid servant."

"He served you faithfully, I am sure; it is not in his nature to be otherwise than faithful in all that he undertakes. He was received here as an equal, and he treated me as such. Neither you nor my mother ever did. I have no memory of one kind look I have received from either of you; and it is hardly to be wondered at that I should have felt grateful to the gentleman who spoke to me in a kind and gentle voice, and who showed in his manner toward me that he regarded me as a lady. He awoke within me a sense of self-respect which might have slept till I was an old woman, whose life, since the death of my father, had never been brightened by a ray of love. He awoke within me, also, a sense of shame; and I saw how humiliating it was that I should be dressed as I am dressed now, in clothes which a common servant would be ashamed to wear. But I had no choice. You gave me food, and you gave me nothing else, not even thanks. You pay your servants wages; you might have paid me something so that I could have bought clothes in which I should not feel degraded. I have not a shilling I can call my own—"

"Don't stop me, Fox," cried Mrs. Fox-Cordery, thoroughly enraged; "I must speak! You shameless creature, how dare you utter these falsehoods? You have a beautiful gown, and a hat, and boots, and everything a woman can wish for; and you stand there, and deny it to my face!"

"I do deny it, mother. Are these things really mine? If they are, why do you keep them locked up in your wardrobe, and why do you allow me to wear them only when I go out with you, or when any particular visitor comes to the house?"

"Because you are not fit to be trusted, you ungrateful child!"

"No, mother, it is not that. You allow me to put them on sometimes because you cannot with decency allow me to be seen as I am. You forget, mother; you have told me over and over again that the clothes I wear—even those I have on now—are not my own, and are only lent to me."

"And so they are. It was not your money that paid for them."

"It could not well have been, seeing I never had any. Will you give them to me to-day, so that I may put them on, and not feel ashamed when I look in the glass?"

"To enable you to go flaunting about, and disgracing yourself and us? No, I will not."

"You are at your shifty tricks again, Charlotte," said Mr. Fox-Cordery. "Finish with your Mr. Dixon."

"Yes, I will do so if you will let me. All the time he was visiting here you said nothing to me to show you did not wish me to be intimate with him."

"We were not aware of what was going on," said Mrs. Fox-Cordery.

"We concealed nothing from you. Three years ago he asked me to be his wife. I answered gladly, yes, and wondered what he could see in me to stoop so low."

"Upon my word!" ejaculated her mother. "And this from a Fox-Cordery!"

"He explained that he was not in good circumstances, and that I would have to wait till he could furnish a home. I said that I would wait for him all my life, and so we were engaged. Then he went from me to you, Fox, and to mother, and asked for your consent."

"And it so happened," said Mr. Fox-Cordery, "that it was the very day on which I discovered that he was not fit to be trusted."

"He is above doing a dishonorable action," said Charlotte, with generous warmth, "and whatever it was you discovered it was not to his discredit."

"That is as good as saying," cried Mrs. Fox-Cordery, advancing a step toward Charlotte, and would have advanced farther if her son had not laid his hand upon her arm, "that the discovery your brother speaks of was to _his_ discredit, and that it was _he_ who was guilty of a dishonorable action. You shall be punished for making these comparisons between your brother and such a creature as Mr. Dixon. My dear Fox, have we not heard enough?"

"No," replied Mr. Fox-Cordery, smiling blandly upon his sister. "We must not give Charlotte the opportunity of saying that she is unfairly treated. Speak freely, Charlotte; you are unbosoming yourself to your best friends. Do not be afraid. We will protect and take care of you. Charlotte harbors none but the most affectionate feelings for us, mother. If in a moment of excitement she says something that is not exactly loving and dutiful, we will excuse her. She will be sorry for it afterward, and that shall be her punishment. Go on, my dear."

"It is scarcely possible," said Charlotte, with a look of repugnance at her brother, "that we can be always right, not even the best of us; sometimes we are mistaken in our judgment, and Fox is when he speaks harshly of Mr. Dixon."

"Convince me of it, my dear," said Mr. Fox-Cordery, nodding genially at her, "and I will make the handsomest apology to him. I will have it written out and illuminated, and he shall hang it, framed, in his room. You cannot complain that I am unfair, after that."

"I was not present when Mr. Dixon spoke to you about our engagement, but I heard high words pass between you."

"Listening at keyholes!" exclaimed Mrs. Fox-Cordery scornfully. "What next?"

"No, no, mother," expostulated Mr. Fox-Cordery; "be just. It was quite natural that Charlotte should listen. Everybody would not have done so, but then Charlotte is not everybody."

"My happiness was at stake," said Charlotte, "and I was anxious."

"You hear, mother. Charlotte was anxious."

"I was not eavesdropping," said Charlotte. "I was downstairs, and your voices forced themselves upon me. Shortly afterward Mr. Dixon came down and told me that there had been a disagreeable scene between you, and that you would not listen to what he had to say about our engagement. 'But I will not give you up,' he said, 'unless you turn away from me.' I answered that it depended upon him, and that I should be very unhappy if our engagement were broken. He said it should not be broken, and that if I would remain true to him he would remain true to me."

"It has a pastoral sound," observed Mr. Fox-Cordery. "Such charming simplicity!"

"He suggested that, before he left the house, we should speak to you together of an agreement we had entered into, and we came up to you. You cannot have forgotten what passed at that interview."

"You were informed that we would not sanction the engagement."

"And Mr. Dixon, speaking for himself and for me, told you that we held to it, and that we had agreed not to think seriously of marriage for three years, during which time he hoped to so improve his position that he would be able to make a home for me. We bound ourselves to this in your presence, and Mr. Dixon said that he would not visit the house without some strong inducement. He has not done so. When he calls this afternoon you will learn why he has come now. During these three years we have corresponded, and have met occasionally in the streets, and have spoken together."

"I believe," remarked Mr. Fox-Cordery, "that servants and their young men are in the habit of meeting in this way."

"I have been no better than a servant," retorted Charlotte, "and many a poor girl has left service to enter into a happy marriage."

"As you are going to do?"

"I do not know. What I wish you and mother to understand is that the three years have expired, and that we do not consider ourselves bound to you any longer."

"Never in the whole course of my life," said Mrs. Fox-Cordery, "did I listen to anything so unladylike and indelicate."

"What it is necessary for you to understand," said Mr. Fox-Cordery, "is that Mr. Dixon will not be permitted to visit you here."

"He will not come to see me here."

"Where, then?"

"I prefer not to tell you."

"You have some idea of a place of meeting?"

"I have something better than an idea, Fox; I have almost a hope."

He repeated her words thoughtfully, "almost a hope," and fixed his eyes upon her face; but he could not read there what he desired to read.

"Have you given any consideration," he asked, "to your circumstances? Do you think that any man would receive you—as you are?"

It was a cruel taunt, and she felt it.

"Yes, I have thought of it," she answered sadly, "and it is a deep trouble to me. If I dared to make an appeal to you—"

"Make it," he said, during the pause that ensued.

"I am your sister, Fox. I have done nothing to disgrace you—nothing of which I should be ashamed. If Mr. Dixon tells me he has a home ready for me, how can I go to him—as I am?"

She looked down at her feet, she spread out her hands piteously, and the tears started to her eyes.

"Well?"

"I think," she said, in an imploring tone, "if father could have seen the future he would have made some provision for me, ever so little, that would enable me to enter a home of my own in a creditable manner."

"What is it, dear Charlotte, that you wish me to do for you?"

"Give me a little money, Fox, to buy a few decent clothes for myself."

"In other words," he said, "furnish you with the means to act in direct opposition to our wishes, to what we are convinced is best for your welfare."

"It is a hard way of expressing it, Fox."

"It is the correct way, Charlotte. I perceive that you are speaking more humbly now. You are not so defiant. You recognize, after all, that you cannot exactly do without us."

"You are my brother. Mother has only you and me."

"Your brother," said Mrs. Fox-Cordery, in a tone of relentless severity, "has been a blessing to me. It is more than I can say of you."

"I have worked hard, mother; I have had few pleasures; I have not cost you much."

"You have cost us too much. We have been overindulgent to you, and in return you insult your brother and set yourself in direct opposition to us. When your father died he left his property wisely. He knew you were not to be trusted; he knew that your ungrateful, willful nature would bring irreparable mischief upon us if it were left uncontrolled. He said as much to me. 'Charlotte will need a strong hand over her,' he said, 'to prevent her bringing shame to your door.'"

"No, no, mother!"

"His very words. I have never repeated them to you because I wished to spare your feelings. 'To prevent her bringing shame to your door. Keep a strict watch over her for all your sakes.' We have done so in fulfillment of our duty, and now it has come to this."

Mr. Fox-Cordery knew that these words had never been uttered by his father, and that there was not a grain of truth in them, but he thoroughly approved of the unworthy device. When he was working to gain a point, there was no trick that was not justifiable in his eyes; and although upon the present occasion he did not exhibit any consciousness of his mother's duplicity, neither of them was deceived by it or ashamed of it.

Charlotte was dismayed by this pretended voice from the grave. Was it possible that it could be true? Had the words really been spoken by the kind father who had left with her a cherished memory of kindness and love? But her experience of her mother was of such a nature that the doubt did not remain long to torture her. She swept it away; and except for the brief period of pain it caused her, it passed, and left no sting behind. She turned to her brother for a response to her appeal.

"Is the hope you referred to," he asked, "the hope of getting money out of me?"

"No," she replied.

"Oblige me by informing me what it is."

"Not till you answer me," she said firmly.

"Take your answer, then. You shall not have a farthing, not one farthing. Now for your hope, please."

"Will nothing move you, Fox?"

"Nothing."

"You leave me no alternative; I must appeal elsewhere. I think I know someone who will extend a helping hand to me. On the few occasions she has been here, and on which you have allowed me to see her, she has spoken to me with such unvarying kindness that I feel confident she will assist me. She has a tender heart, I am sure, and she will feel for me. I hope you will be happy with her; I hope it from my heart--"

She was not allowed to finish. Her brother, striding forward, seized her by the wrist so fiercely that she gave utterance to a cry of pain. The next moment she released herself—not a difficult matter, for, woman as she was, her strength exceeded his. Mr. Fox-Cordery had so effectually schooled himself that he had an almost perfect command over his features, and it was seldom that he was so forgetful as to show the fury of his soul. Even now, when a tempest was raging within him, there was little indication of it in his face, and but for the glittering of his blue eyes there was no evidence of his agitation. In a cold voice he said:

"No further subterfuge. Name the lady."

"Mrs. Grantham."

Mr. Fox-Cordery and his mother exchanged glances.

"Do you mean," he asked, "that you would go to her and beg?"

"I would go to her," replied Charlotte, "and relate the story of my life—of my outward and inward life, Fox—from beginning to end. If I do, it will be you who drive me to it."

"We now fully realize, my dear mother," said Mr. Fox-Cordery, seating himself and crossing his legs, "Charlotte's character. At length she has revealed her true nature."

"I have nourished a serpent in my bosom," said Mrs. Fox-Cordery.

"She would destroy the hope of my life," continued Mr. Fox-Cordery; "she would blight my happiness forever. Knowing that I love the lady she has named, and that it is the one wish of my heart to make her my wife, she would deliberately blacken my character with her lies, and, under the pretense of a womanly appeal to that lady's feelings, would do her best to wreck my future."

"If my cause is not a just one," said Charlotte, "no appeal of mine will avail with Mrs. Grantham. God forbid that I should step between you and her; but I have my future to look to, as you have yours, and I am weary of the life I have led. A happier life is offered to me, and I cannot relinquish it at your bidding without an effort. If I tamely submitted to your will I should be unworthy of the gentleman who has honored me with his love."

"We will leave that gentleman, as you call him, out of the question. The contention lies between you and me, and I am free to confess that you have the advantage of me. I am no match for you, Charlotte. You are far too clever and cunning for me, and the feelings I entertain for the lady whose name has been dragged into this unhappy discussion place me at your mercy. I have made no secret of these feelings; I have foolishly bared my breast to you and you tread upon it. I yield; I hold out a flag of truce. You will give me time to consider your proposition? It comes upon me as a surprise, you know. I was not prepared for it."

"Yes, Fox, I will give you time," said Charlotte, somewhat bewildered at finding herself master of the situation. She had not expected so sudden a victory. "But there is one thing I wish you would ask mother to do at once."

"What is it, Charlotte?"

"Let me have my clothes that are in her wardrobe. I am wretched and miserable in these."

"You will give them to her, mother," said Mr. Fox-Cordery; and his mother, taking the cue, replied:

"She can have them; I have only kept them in my room to take proper care of them."

"There, Charlotte, you have nothing now to complain of."

"But you have not answered me yet, Fox," said Charlotte, resolved not to lose sight of the main point.

"About the money you ask for? May I inquire if you are in a great hurry to get married?"

"I am not in a great hurry, Fox," said Charlotte rather awkwardly. "It rests with Mr. Dixon."

"What does he say about it?"

"He thinks we might get married in two or three months."

"There is no particular hurry, then; we have time before us to conquer the repugnance we feel toward him. After all, it will make you happier if you marry with our sanction."

"Much happier, Fox."

"Mother and I will talk over the matter together dispassionately, and if we can bring ourselves to look upon him with friendly eyes we will do so. That is fair speaking, is it not?"

"Yes," said Charlotte, hesitating a little, "I think so."

She was drifting from the advantageous position she had gained, and she was weakly sensible of it; but her brother's manner was so conciliatory, and her own desire for peace so strong, that she could scarcely help herself.

"The money you require is not required immediately, and just now I am rather embarrassed with calls upon me. You would not wish to injure me financially, Charlotte?"

"No, Fox; indeed I would not."

"Everything will come right," said Mr. Fox-Cordery. "In a month or two I hope to set myself straight. Meanwhile, as we have agreed, we will enter into a truce. There shall be no more unpleasantnesses between us. We have had a family disagreement, that is all; I blow it away." He made a motion with his lips, as though he were blowing away a cloud. "So, for two months, we will say nothing more concerning the affair. If you have had something to complain of in the past, it is perhaps due to the anxieties by which I have been overwhelmed. You do not know what a man's troubles are, fighting with the world and with people who are trying to get the advantage of him. Be thankful that you are a woman, and are spared these trials. You shall have nothing to complain of in the future."

"Thank you, Fox."

"I have your promise, Charlotte, that the matter shall rest for two months, when, no doubt, you will have everything you wish for."

"Yes, I promise," said Charlotte, feeling rather helpless.

"And you will say nothing to Mrs. Grantham about our little disagreement till that time has expired, when there will be no occasion whatever to humiliate yourself and us? That, of course, is agreed."

"Yes, Fox."

"It is a sacred promise, mind."

"I have given it, and I will keep to it."

"Very well; we are good friends again, and always shall be. By the way, Charlotte, I am going to take a house on the Thames for the summer months."

"I heard mother mention it."

"Partly to give you some pleasure and relaxation. We will have pleasant times there."

"I hope so, Fox."

"Mother," said Mr. Fox-Cordery, as if the idea had just occurred to him, instead of having been in his mind for several weeks, "you might invite Mrs. Grantham to pay us a visit there, and to remain with us a little while. It will be company for Charlotte."

"I will write to-day if you wish, my love," said Mrs. Fox-Cordery, responding to his suggestion immediately, as she always did. These two perfectly understood each other.

"Not to-day, mother; we must wait till I have taken the house. The one you spoke of will do capitally, if it answers to the description in the letter. And, Charlotte, when mother writes to Mrs. Grantham, you might write also, saying how glad you will be if she comes to us—a nice letter, Charlotte, with as many pretty things in it as you can think of. You see the confidence I place in you, my dear."

"I will write when you tell me, Fox. It will be a great pleasure to me if she comes."

"That is what I want—to give you as much pleasure as possible. Now, my dear, go to your room. I am very glad our little misunderstanding has ended so amicably."

He smiled affection upon Charlotte, and she left mother and son together. For a few moments there was silence—he chewing the cud of savage reflection, she throbbing with affection for him and with anger at her daughter's presumption.

"What made you so smooth with her, Fox?" asked Mrs. Fox-Cordery.

"It was the only way to muzzle her," he replied. "If she had done what she threatened it would have ruined all."

"She would never have dared," said Mrs. Fox-Cordery.

"She would have dared, egged on by that scoundrel Dixon, and by her love for him."

"Love!" muttered Mrs. Fox-Cordery, contemptuously.

"Or what she fancies is love; but I think she really loves the man, and I know what love will dare."

"For Heaven's sake," exclaimed Mrs. Fox-Cordery, "don't institute comparisons between you and her! She is not fit to black your shoes."

"She has polished them often enough," he remarked grimly; "but that is coming to an end now. A good job; I'm sick of the sight of her; I'm sick of myself; I'm sick of everything, and everybody."

"Not everybody, my love," she said, placing her hand on his shoulder fondly.

He shook her off, and she did not murmur. They resembled each other most wonderfully, but there was a marked difference in the quality of their affection. She—cold, hard, and ungenerous to all but him—was nobler than he, for she was ready and willing to sacrifice herself for him. It had been so from his birth, and her love had grown into a passion which nothing could affect, not even ingratitude and indifference from the son she adored. In her eyes he was a paragon; his vices were virtues, his meanness commendable, his trickery the proof of an ingenious mind. He could do no wrong. Quick to discover the least sign of turpitude in others, she discerned none in him; she was morally blind to his defects, and the last thing she would have believed him capable of was the Judas kiss.

Far different was it with him. He was conscious of all his mother's faults, and he excused her for none. His absorbing vanity so clouded his mind that it was only the baser qualities of those with whom he was associated that forced themselves upon his attention, and these being immediately accepted the door was closed upon the least attribute which rendered them worthy of respect and esteem. His chronic suspicion of his fellow-creatures did not spring from his intellect, but from those lower conditions of the affections in which the basest qualities of mankind occupy the prominent places. Theophrastus says that the suspicious man imputes a fraudulent intention to everyone with whom he has to do, and this was the case with Mr. Fox-Cordery, who viewed his mother—the one being in the world who, though he stood universally condemned and execrated, would have shed the last drop of her blood in his defense and vindication—in the same light as he viewed those who were as ready to spurn him in the day of his prosperity as in the day of his downfall, should such a day ever dawn upon him.

"Follow my lead," he said to his mother, "in your treatment of Charlotte. She has declared war, and war it shall be, though she shall not see it till the proper time. Just now she is necessary to me. Strange as it may sound, her good word will be of assistance to me with Mrs. Grantham. I cannot account for it, and I am not going to trouble myself about it; the only thing that troubles me is that the lady I have loved for so many years should still hold off, should still refuse to speak the word that will make me happy. What am I taking a country house for except to further the dearest wish of my heart? I think of no one but her; I dream of no one but her. She was snatched from me once, and I had to bear it; and then fortune declared itself in my favor, and still I could not obtain the prize I have been so long working for."

"You are a model of constancy, my love," said his mother, affectionately and admiringly. "No woman in the world is good enough for my dear son."

"Perhaps not, perhaps not," he muttered; "but I will die before I am thwarted. When did I give up an object upon which I set my heart? Never, and I will not give up this. Mark the hour that makes Mrs. Grantham my wife, and you will see me a changed man. She shall be my slave then, as I am hers now. During her visit to us I will conquer her irresolution, her obstinacy. Let Charlotte understand that her happiness depends upon mine; that will win her completely to my side. I will be the most affectionate of brothers; you shall be the most affectionate of mothers. Charlotte will say to herself, 'I have been mistaken in them; it is I who have been at fault all these years.' This will tell in my favor when she and Mrs. Grantham are talking together confidentially. We rob her, you see, of her power of detraction. You, I know, will do your best, and Charlotte shall do her best instead of her worst. She has defied me; she shall be made to pay for it. I have her promise for two months, and she is at my mercy. Do you understand now why I was so smooth with her?"

"Yes, my love. Depend upon me to do everything in my power."

"Before those two months have gone Mrs. Grantham and I shall be man and wife; and then, mother, Charlotte may go to the—"

"Exactly so, my love," said his mother.

CHAPTER V.

In which John Dixon informs Mr. Fox-Cordery that he has seen a Ghost.

It is an article of belief that every Englishman's private residence must include an apartment which, by a polite fiction, is denominated a study. This apartment, which generally smells of musty bones, is, as a rule, extremely small, extremely dark, and extremely useless. Dust lies thick upon the shabby furniture, by reason of the housemaid never being allowed to enter it with duster and broom; and the few volumes on the shelves of the parody of a bookcase lean against each other at a drunken angle, with a dissipated air of books that have lost all respect for themselves. To add to the conspicuous cheerlessness of the room, its one insufficient window looks out upon a dreary back wall, a constant contemplation of which would be likely to drive a man's thoughts in the direction of suicide. Provided with the necessary cupboard, no more suitable hiding-place could be found for the proverbial family skeleton, without which no well-regulated establishment can be said to be complete.

Into such an apartment was John Dixon shown when he was informed that Mr. Fox-Cordery would receive him.

This cold welcome was a sufficient indication that the master of the house did not regard his visitor in the light of a friend; but, clear as was the fact to John Dixon, it did not disturb him. With his rubicund face, his bright eyes, and his genial manners, he presented the appearance of a man not easily disturbed, of a man who accepted the rubs of life with equanimity, and made the best of them. He was in his prime, a well-built gentleman, with nothing particularly serious on his conscience, and when Mr. Fox-Cordery entered the room the advantage was on John Dixon's side, physically and morally.

They glanced at each other inquiringly, and with a certain curiosity, for it was long since they had met face to face. Mr. Fox-Cordery was disappointed; he had hoped to see signs of wear and tear in his old friend, in the shape of crows'-feet, wrinkles, and gray hairs, but none were visible. On the contrary, there was an assertion of robust youth and good health about John Dixon which gave positive pain to Mr. Fox-Cordery.

"Good-day, Fox," said John Dixon cordially.

Mr. Fox-Cordery did not respond to the salutation. Stiffening his little body—an action which brought a broad smile to John Dixon's lips—he said in his iciest tone:

"To what may I ascribe the—"

"The honor of this visit," broke in John Dixon heartily. "I'll come to it soon. You don't seem comfortable, Fox."

"Whether I am comfortable or not," said Mr. Fox-Cordery, who would have administered a dose of poison to his visitor with the greatest pleasure in life, "cannot possibly concern or interest you."

"Oh! but I beg your pardon. Everything appertaining to Charlotte's brother must concern and interest me. It stands to reason. We shall one day be brothers-in-law. Brothers-in-law! Good Lord! Don't shift your legs so, Fox. Keep still and straight, as you were a moment ago. To a little man like you repose is invaluable."

"Your familiarity, Mr. Dixon—"

"Come, come," interrupted John Dixon, with a genial shake of his head; "why not John? I shall not take offense at it."

"Have you paid me an unwelcome visit to force a quarrel upon me?"

"By no means. I know that my visit is an unwelcome one. You don't like my company, Fox."

"Your room would be preferable."

"It is a treat to hear something honest from you. There, there, man, don't fume! You can't alter me any more than I can alter you. What is bred in the bone, you know. And let me tell you, Fox, you can't expect to have everything your own way. Who plays at bowls must be prepared for rubbers."

"Let me tell _you_, Mr. Dixon," said Mr. Fox-Cordery, becoming suddenly calm, "that I will submit to none of your impertinence."

He was about to continue in this strain when he suddenly recollected that he had assumed a new attitude toward Charlotte, and that, if her lover represented to her that he had been insulted by him, it might interfere with his plans. It was advisable, therefore, that not a word that passed at the present interview should reach Charlotte's ears, and he saw a way to compass this. Changing front instantly, he said slyly:

32

"I should like to know if we are speaking in confidence?"

"In strict confidence," said John Dixon readily. "For your sake, Fox, not for mine."

"Never mind for whose sake. You have your opinions, I have mine. I take your word, and shall be outspoken with you. You had the presumption to pay a visit to my sister this morning—"

"No, no, Fox, to you; though I must confess I was delighted to see her, and have a chat with her."

"It was for that purpose you came. As we have met in perfect confidence, and as nothing that we say to each other will be repeated by either of us outside this room—that is a perfectly honorable engagement, is it not?"

"It is on my side," said John Dixon gravely.

"I have bound myself, Mr. Dixon, and am therefore free to warn you that you must cease from persecuting Charlotte with your addresses. I speak in her name."

"Not true, Fox; you speak in your own. Why, if she herself uttered those words to me I should not believe they came from her heart; I should know that you forced her to speak them. But there is no fear of anything of that sort occurring. Charlotte and I understand each other; and, oppressed and ground down as she has been in your house, she has a higher courage than you give her credit for. I am proud of having won her love, and I will make her a happy woman, as truly as I stand here. However, it is not to tell you what you already know that I have come to see you; it is for a different reason altogether."

"You speak defiantly, Mr. Dixon. It is not the way to conciliate me."

"Conciliate you! I am not such an ass as to try. I will try my own way. If I can manage it, you shall fear me."

"If you can manage it!" said Mr. Fox-Cordery, a little uneasy at his visitor's confident tone. "Yes, if you can manage it. I should imagine you will find it a difficult task. If you think you can frighten me by your bullying you are mistaken."

"Oh! I don't want to frighten you. I am going to play my cards openly, knowing perfectly well that you will not expose one of yours. Shall we proceed to business?"

"Say what you have to say," exclaimed Mr. Fox-Cordery blandly, "and the devil take you!"

John Dixon laughed.

"When you speak softly, Fox, you are most deadly. It was just the same when you, I, and Robert Grantham were at school together in the country. Poor Bob! What a careless, reckless, generous fellow he was! What a tool he was in your hands, and how you worked him and played upon him!"

"You lie," said Mr. Fox-Cordery, in a passionless voice.

Few persons acquainted with him would have suspected how deeply he was agitated by this reference to his old schoolmate.

"The scapegoat of the school," proceeded John Dixon, as if Mr. Fox-Cordery had not spoken. "As easily led as a fly in harness. We three were differently circumstanced. My people were poor, and could allow me very little pocket-money; Bob Grantham's people were rich, and he had a liberal supply. What your people allowed you no one knew. You kept your affairs very secret, Fox; you were always a sly, vain, cautious customer. Poor Bob was the soul of frankness; he made no secret of anything, not even of his weaknesses, which he laughed at as freely as some others did. Regularly every fourth Monday his foolish people sent him ten pounds, and quite as regularly on the very next day he had not a penny of his ten pounds left. Where did his money go to? Who, in the course of a few short hours, had got hold of it? Some said he gave it away to any poor man or woman he happened to meet. Some said he chucked it into the pond out of dare-devilry. When he was questioned, he turned it off with a laugh. You used to be asked about it, and you used to answer, 'How should I know?' It was a mystery, and Bob never blabbed—nor did you, Fox!"

"How could I supply information," said Mr. Fox-Cordery, "upon a matter so mysterious; and what is the meaning of all this rhodomontade?"

"I suppose," continued John Dixon, still as if Mr. Fox-Cordery had not spoken, "that most boys set up for themselves a code of honor which they stick to, more or less, according to their idea of things. I remember I did; I am quite sure poor Bob Grantham did; I don't know whether you did, because you were so secretive, so very secretive. I leave you out, Fox, for a cogent reason. I guess, as our American cousins say, you are not in it when I speak of honor; and in making this observation you will perceive that I have no desire to conciliate you or to win your favor. Now, old fellow, there were only three boys in the whole of that school—and there were thirty-five of us—who knew what became of Bob Grantham's money."

"Three persons!"

"Just three persons, and no more. The first was poor Bob himself, the second was Fox-Cordery, the third was John Dixon."

"Indeed! You?"

"I, on the honor of a gentleman."

Mr. Fox-Cordery's lips curled in derision as he remarked:

"No man in the world would give you the credit of being one. And pray, where did Mr. Grantham's money go to?"

"Into your pockets, Fox, as regularly as a clockwork machine."

"A precious secret, truly," said Mr. Fox-Cordery, flicking a speck of dust off his sleeve, "and a most valuable one for you to have preserved all these years. I presume if a man, or a schoolboy, is weak enough to lend his money he has a right to receive it back."

"An indubitable right; but in this case there is no question of borrowing and paying back. Would you like to hear how I came into a knowledge of this mystery?"

"I have no desire; it is quite immaterial to me."

"It was an accidental discovery. You and Bob Grantham were bosom friends. It was touching to observe how deeply attached you were to him; and, in these circumstances, any friendship he formed being on his part sincere, it was natural that you should be much in each other's society. Now, it was noticeable that every fourth Monday evening you and he disappeared for an hour or two, and it was for this reason that you used to be asked what Bob Grantham did with the ten pounds he received regularly on that day. On one of these Monday evenings I happened to be taking a lonely walk in a pretty bit of forest about two miles from the schoolhouse. There was a nook in the forest which was very secluded, and one had to go out of one's way to get to it. I went out of my way on that particular Monday evening, not because I wanted to reach this secluded nook, because I did not know of it, but aimlessly and without any special purpose. I heard voices, and peeping through a cluster of trees, I saw you and Bob sitting on the grass, playing cards. A white handkerchief was spread between you, and on this handkerchief were the stakes you were playing for—Bob's money and your own. I waited, and observed. Sovereign after sovereign went into your pocket. You were quiet, and cool, and bland, as you are now, though I dare say something is passing inside of you. What a rare power you have of concealing your feelings, Fox! Some people might envy you; I don't. Bob Grantham, all the time he was losing, laughed and joked, and bore his losses like a man; and he kept on losing till he was cleaned out. Then he rose, and laughingly said: 'You will give me my revenge, Fox?' 'When you like, old fellow,' you answered; 'what bad luck you have.' 'Oh, it will turn,' he said; 'all you've got to do is to stick to it.' That is how I discovered where poor Bob's money went to, Fox."

"Well, and what of it?" said Mr. Fox-Cordery, with a sneer. "He was fond of a game of cards, and he played and lost. That there was nothing wrong in it was proved by your silence. And that is what you have come here to-day to tell me! You are a fool for your pains, John Dixon."

"I was silent," said John Dixon, "because Bob pledged me to secrecy. My intention was to expose you to the whole school, and so put an end to—what shall we call it? Robbery?"

"You would not dare to make that charge against me in public. There are no witnesses present, and you, therefore, know you are protected against an action for libel."

"You are losing sight of your compact of silence, Fox. Tiled in as we are, we can call each other what names we please, and there is no obligation upon us to be choice in our language. Pull yourself together, my little man; I have no desire to take you at a disadvantage. What do you say, now, to our agreeing that this meeting shall not be confidential, and that when we part we shall each of us be free to reveal what passes?"

"My word once given," replied Mr. Fox-Cordery, putting on his loftiest air, "I never depart from it."

"For all that," said John Dixon, "I will give you the opportunity of challenging me in public, and of seeing whether I will not give you the chance of bringing an action for libel against me. Having made up my mind what to do I considered it right to tell Bob of my intention. He turned white with anger; he called me a treacherous dog; he said that I had sneaked my way into a secret which had nothing whatever to do with me, and that I should be playing a base part by revealing it. We had some warm words about you, Fox, and he defended you tooth and nail. Upon my word, after our quarrel I had a greater admiration for poor Bob than ever. The end of it was that he bound me down, upon honor, to keep the secret from any but our three selves, and that is why it never leaked out."

"Mr. Grantham had his good points," observed Mr. Fox-Cordery; "there was something of the gentleman in him; that is why I chummed with him. May I inquire how it was that, entertaining such an opinion of me, you, a good many years after we all left school, accepted the offer of employment I made you—which never would have been made, I need hardly say, if I had known you then as I know you now?"

"I was down in the world; things had gone badly with me, and it was necessary for me to get something to do without delay. You are aware that I have an old mother to support: and when needs must—I need not finish the old saying. When, meeting by chance, as we did, you made me the offer, I did not tell you I was in low water, or you would have screwed me down without mercy. I intended to remain with you only long enough to save a few pounds, but getting to know Charlotte, and growing fond of her, I could not tear myself away from her. I will continue the story of poor Bob. The discovery I made did not alter things in the least; it rather improved them for you. Bob and you became more and more attached to each other, and you left school firm friends. I never could understand what he saw in you, but you have the faculty of inspiring confidence in some people—worse luck for them in the long run."

"I am waiting for your insults to come to an end," said Mr. Fox-Cordery, "and to have the pleasure of hearing the street door close on you."

"All in good time, Fox; I told you I should not try conciliatory methods. Our school-days over, we lost sight of each other, that is to say, I lost sight of you and Bob, and what I have now to speak of has come to my knowledge in various ways. After leaving school a series of family adventures befell Robert Grantham. His parents died, his elder brother died, a rich uncle died, and to Bob's share fell a larger fortune than he expected to inherit. His good luck must have bewildered him, for he appointed you his agent. The next point of interest to touch upon is the introduction of a lady in your lives. Her maiden name, Lucy Sutherland. Correct me if I am making any misstatement."

"I decline to make myself responsible for any statement of yours, whether it be correct or otherwise. Your introduction of this lady's name is a gross impertinence."

"Not at all; it belongs to the story, which, without it, is incomplete. I have not the pleasure of this lady's acquaintance, and, to my knowledge, have never seen her, but I have heard of her, through you and Charlotte."

"Through me!"

"To be sure," continued John Dixon, "you never mentioned her to me by that name, but by the name she now bears, Mrs. Grantham. Probably you would never have mentioned her to me at all had it not been that she was concerned in the business you set me to do during my service with you. You had the management of her financial affairs, as you had the management of her husband's. But I am running ahead of my story. As a maiden lady she had many suitors, which is not to be wondered at, for though she had terrible anxieties and trials she is still, as I learn from Charlotte, very beautiful, and as good as she is beautiful. I trust Charlotte's judgment in this as in all things. Only two of these suitors for her hand did Miss Sutherland smile upon. One was poor Bob Grantham, the other yourself. But you did not hold an equal place in her regard. She smiled upon poor Bob because she loved him, she smiled upon you because you were the bosom friend of the gentleman she loved. Into the sincerity of your feelings for her I do not inquire; I pass over what does not concern me, and I come to the commencement of an important chapter in this lady's life, which opens with her marriage with Robert Grantham."

"You pass over what does not concern you," said Mr. Fox-Cordery. "What, then, is your object in dragging the lady's name into the conversation?"

"You will learn presently. The chapter opens brightly, but we have only to turn a leaf and we see clouds gathering. Mark you; from all I can gather these two loved each other with a very perfect love; but poor Bob had one besetting vice which darkened his life and hers, and which eventually ruined both. He was an inveterate gamester. The seeds of this vice, which you helped to nourish in our school days, were firmly implanted in him when he grew to manhood. He was, as I have already said, weak, and easily led, and no doubt the harpies who are always on the watch for such as he encouraged him and fattened upon him. He had not the strength to withstand temptation, and he fell lower and lower. Observe, Fox, that in the narration of the story I am merely giving you a plain recital of facts."

"Or what you suppose to be facts," interrupted Mr. Fox-Cordery.

"A plain recital of facts," repeated John Dixon, "the truth of which can be substantiated. I do not ask you whether you took a hand in poor Bob's ruin, and profited by it. That some harpies did is not to be doubted, because in the end poor Bob lost every penny of his fortune, which all found its way into their pockets, as the weak schoolboy's ten pounds found their way regularly every month into yours. I do not seek to excuse poor Bob; there is a thin line which separates weakness and folly from sin, and Bob was one of the many who stepped over this line. I have reflected deeply upon his wretched history. Knowing the goodness of his heart and the sweetness of his disposition, I have wondered how he could have been so blind as not to see that he was breaking the heart of the woman he loved and had sworn to protect; her nature must also have been one of rare goodness that she did not force it upon him, that she did not take the strongest means to show him the miserable pit he was digging for them. I have wondered, too, how, through another influence than that of his wife, he himself should not have awakened from his fatal infatuation. They had a child, a little girl, and his instinctive tenderness for children should have stepped in to save him. I am not myself a gambler, and I cannot realize the complete power which the vice obtains over a man's moral perception, sapping all that is noble and worthy in him, and destroying all the finer instincts of his nature. Happily Mrs. Grantham had a fortune in her own right over which her husband had no control; some portion of it went, I believe, to save him from disgrace—and then the end came. I have related the story in its broad outlines; there must have been scenes of agony between husband and wife of which I know nothing, but it is not difficult to imagine them. During the whole of these miserable years, Fox, you remained the close friend and associate of this unhappy couple, and you know what the end of it was."

"What I know I know," said Mr. Fox-Cordery, "and I do not propose to enlist you in my confidence."

"I do not ask you to do so. It was probably during these years that Mrs. Grantham learned to rely upon you and to trust to your counsel and judgment. You have maintained your position to this day."

"Well?"

"In the course of the business I transacted for you I became somewhat familiar with Mrs. Grantham's pecuniary affairs. You are, in a certain sense, her trustee and guardian; you have the management of her little fortune; it was partly with respect to the investments you made for her that we severed our connection."

"That I dismissed you from my service," corrected Mr. Fox-Cordery. "You had the presumption to suppose that you had the right to interfere in my management. I opened your eyes to your position, and sent you packing."

"As it suited me to accept employment when you offered it to me, so it suited me to leave your service at the time I did. A better situation was open to me, with the prospect of a future partnership. On the day I left you I went to my new situation, and have been in it ever since. In a short time I shall become a partner in the firm of Paxton and Freshfield, solicitors, Bedford Row."

"It is not of the slightest interest to me, Mr. Dixon, whether you become a partner in this firm or go to the dogs. I can forecast which of the two is the more likely."

"Had you the disposition of my future I know pretty well what it would be; but I promise you disappointment. Although you take no interest in the circumstances of my becoming a partner in Paxton and Freshfield I will leave our address with you, in case you may wish to consult me."

He laid a card upon the table, of which Mr. Fox-Cordery took no notice.

"This, then," he said, "is the reason of your intrusion. To solicit my patronage? You would have made a good commercial traveler."

"You are miles from the truth. I do not think we would undertake your business. I leave my card for private, not for professional reasons. What I have stated to you leads directly to the object of my visit. I have hitherto asked you no questions; perhaps you will not object to my asking you one or two now?"

"Say what you please. I can answer or not, at my discretion."

"Entirely so; and pray take it from me that I am not here in a professional capacity, but solely as a private individual who will certainly at no distant date be a member of your family, whether you like it or not; or," he added, with a slight laugh, "whether I like it or not. In conveying to you my regret that I shall have a relationship thrust upon me which I would very gladly dispense with, my reference is not to Charlotte. A relationship to you, apart from other considerations, is no credit; but, so far as Charlotte and I are concerned, I would prefer it without the additional drawback of a public scandal. Many singular pieces of business fall into the hands of Paxton and Freshfield. One of such a nature came into the office a short time since, but it was not brought before my notice till to-day. Have you seen the _Times_ this morning?"

"I decline to answer idle questions."

"Whether you have seen it or not, an advertisement in its personal columns has certainly escaped your attention, or you would not have met this particular question so calmly. The advertisement, as you will see—I have brought the paper with me—was inserted by my firm. It will interest you to read it."

He took the _Times_ from his pocket, and offered it to Mr. Fox-Cordery, pointing to the advertisement of which he spoke; Mr. Fox-Cordery hesitated a moment, and then, paper in hand, stepped to the dusty window, and read the advertisement, which ran as follows:

If Mr. Robert Grantham, born in Leamington, Warwickshire, will call upon Messrs. Paxton and Freshfield, solicitors, Bedford Row, London, he will hear of something to his advantage.

To read so short an advertisement would occupy a man scarcely half a minute, but Mr. Fox-Cordery stood for several minutes at the window, with his back turned to John Dixon. Perhaps there was something in the prospect of the dreary back wall that interested him, for he stood quite still, and did not speak. His contemplation at an end, he faced his visitor, and handed back the paper.

"Have you anything to remark?" inquired John Dixon.

"Nothing."

"Close as wax, Fox, as usual. When I read the advertisement this morning it gave me a strange turn, and I came direct to your house to speak to you about it. Before I did so, I made myself acquainted with the nature of the business concerning which our firm desires to see Mr. Robert Grantham. It is a simple matter enough. An old lady has died in Leamington; she was aunt to poor Bob, and she has left him a small legacy of two hundred pounds. Not a fortune, but a useful sum to a man in low water."

"You are talking rubbish," said Mr. Fox-Cordery. "You know perfectly well that it is throwing money away to put such an advertisement in the papers. Is it in other papers as well as the _Times?_ "

"Ah, ha, friend Fox!" said John Dixon. "Caught tripping for once. Actually betraying interest in the object of my visit, when indifference was your proper cue! No, it is not in other papers; the whole of the small legacy must not be eaten up in expenses. Had I been informed of this business before the insertion of the advertisement even in one paper, I should have suggested to Paxton and Freshfield the advisability of a little delay until I had made certain inquiries. Lawyers are practical people, and they would have recognized the absurdity of inviting by public proclamation a visit from a ghost. There is no mistake, I suppose, about poor Bob being dead?"

"You know he is dead."

"Softly, Fox, softly. I know nothing of poor Bob except what I have gathered from you. If Mrs. Grantham is a widow, why of course Robert Grantham is a dead man; if she is not a widow, why of course Robert Grantham is alive, and you stand small chance of stepping into his shoes, which I believe you are eager to do. It is hardly likely that she has seen the advertisement, but it must be brought to her notice very soon."

"By whom?"

"Naturally, in the first place, by you, as her business agent, because, in the event of Bob being dead, the legacy will fall to his heirs. Failing you, naturally by Paxton and Freshfield, who have this inconsiderable business in hand, and whose duty it is to attend to it. Probably we shall await some communication from you or Mrs. Grantham upon the matter. It may be that Paxton and Freshfield will expect something from you in the shape of a document, such, for instance, as proof of poor Bob's death; and they might consider it advisable to ask for certain particulars, such as the place and date of his death, where buried, etcetera. All of which you will be able to supply, being positive that Mrs. Grantham is a widow. Now, Fox, I have still a word or two to say to you in private. Call it an adventure, an impression, what you will; it occurred to me, and it would be unfair to keep it from Charlotte's brother. Until to-day I have not mentioned it to a soul. We have passed through a hard winter, as you know, and have established a record in fogs. I do not remember a year in which we have had so many foggy days and nights, and the month of March usurped the especial privilege of the month of November. I cannot recall the precise date, but it was about the middle of March when I walked from the Strand into Regent Street by way of the Seven Dials. It was one of the foggiest nights we had, and I had to be careful how I picked my steps. Men walked a yard or two ahead of you, and you could not see their faces, could scarcely distinguish their forms; but quite close, elbow to elbow, as it were, you might by chance catch a momentary glance of a face. A flash, and it was gone, swallowed up in Egyptian darkness. Two men passed me arm-in-arm, and, looking up, I could have sworn that I saw the face of Robert Grantham's ghost. I turned to follow it, but it was gone. That is all, Fox; I thought you would like to know."

If a face of the pallid hue of Mr. Fox-Cordery's could be said to grow white, it may be said of his at this revelation; otherwise he betrayed no sign of agitation. He made no comment upon it, and asked no questions; but the indefinite change of color did not escape John Dixon's observation.

"It is a pleasure to know that you have emptied your budget," he said. "Good-morning, Mr. Dixon."

"Good-morning, Fox," said John Dixon. "You will probably acknowledge that I had a sufficient reason for paying you this visit."

He did not wait for the acknowledgment, but took his departure without another word.

Mr. Fox-Cordery stood motionless by the window. There was writing on the dreary back wall, invisible to all eyes but his.

"If he has betrayed me!" he muttered; "if he has betrayed me!" and pursued his thought no further in spoken words.

A quarter of an hour afterward he went to his mother.

"Have you given Charlotte her clothes?" he asked.

"Not yet, Fox," she replied. "What did that man want with you?"

"That man is my enemy!" he said, with fury in his voice and face; "my bitter enemy. Go, and give Charlotte her clothes immediately. And, mother, take her out and buy her one or two nicknacks—a silver brooch for a few shillings, a bit of ribbon. Be sweet to her. Curse her and him! Be sweet to her, and say I gave you the money to buy the presents. We need her on our side more than ever. Don't stop to argue with me; do as I bid you!"

"I will obey you in everything, my love," she said, gazing at him solicitously.

He motioned her away, and she stole from the room, wishing she possessed the malignant power to strike his enemy dead at her feet.

CHAPTER VI.

In which we make the acquaintance of Rathbeal.

That same night, as Big Ben was striking the hour of nine, Mr. Fox-Cordery, spick and span as usual, and with not a visible crease upon him, crossed Westminster Bridge, Kennington way, bent on an errand of importance, and plunged into the melancholy thoroughfares which beset, but cannot be said to adorn, that sad-colored neighborhood. In some quarters of London the houses have a peculiarly forlorn appearance, as though life at its best were a poor thing, and not worth troubling about. If general cheerlessness and despondency had been the aim of the builders and speculators responsible for their distinguishing characteristics, they may be complimented upon their success, but certainly not upon their taste. It is as easy to make houses pretty as to make them ugly, and curves are no more difficult to compass than angles; facts which have not established themselves in the consciousness of the average Englishman, who remains stupidly content with dull, leaden-looking surfaces, and a pernicious uniformity of front—which may account for the dejection of visage to be met with in such streets as Mr. Fox-Cordery was traversing.

He paid no attention to the typical signs, animate or inanimate, he met with on his road, but walked straight on till he arrived at a three-storied house, in the windows of which not a glimmer of light was to be seen. Striking a match, he held it up to the knocker of the street door, beneath which the number of the house was painted in fast-fading figures; and convincing himself with some difficulty that he had reached his destination, he put his hand to the knocker to summon the inmates. But the knocker had seen its best days, and was almost past knocking. Rust and age had so stiffened its joints that it required a determined effort to move it from its cushion; and being moved, there it stuck in mid-air, obstinately declining to perform its office.

Failing to produce a sound that would have any effect upon human ears, Mr. Fox-Cordery turned his attention to the bells, of which there were six or seven. As there was no indication of the particular bell which would serve him, he pulled them all, one after the other. Some were mute, some gave forth the faintest tinkle, and one remained in his hand, refusing to come farther forward or to go back; the result of his pulling being that not the slightest attention was paid to the summons by anyone in the house. The appearance of a hobbledehoy promised to be of assistance to him. This hobbledehoy was a stripling of same thirteen summers; his shirt-sleeves turned(?) up, and he carried in his hand a pewter pot of beer which he occasionally put his lips, not daring to go deeper than the froth, from fear of consequences from the lawful owner.

"Mr. Rathbeal lives here, doesn't he?" inquired Mr. Fox-Cordery.

The hobbledehoy surveyed the gentleman, and became instantly lost in admiration. Such a vision of perfect dressing had probably never presented itself to him before. Open-mouthed he gazed and worshiped. Mr. Fox-Cordery aroused him from his dream by repeating the question.

"Lots o' people lives 'ere," he replied. "Who's Mr. What's-his-name, when he's at 'ome, and does 'is mother know he's out when he ain't?"

Mr. Fox-Cordery spelt the name, letter by letter—"R-a-t-h-b-e-a-l."

"Don't know the gent," said the hobbledehoy. "Is he a sport?"

No, Mr. Fox-Cordery could not say he was a sport.

"Is he a coster?"

No, Mr. Fox-Cordery could not say he was a coster.

"Is it sweeps?"

No, Mr. Fox-Cordery could not say it was sweeps.

"Give it up," said the hobbledehoy. "Arsk me another."

Another did not readily present itself to Mr. Fox-Cordery's usually fertile mind, and he stood irresolute.

"I tell yer wot," suggested the hobbledehoy. "Give me tuppence, and I'll go through the lot."

With a wry face, Mr. Fox-Cordery produced the coppers, which the hobbledehoy spun in the air, and pocketed. Then he conscientiously went through the list of the inmates of the house from basement to attic, Mr. Fox-Cordery shaking his head at each introduction.

"There's the gent with the 'air on," he said, in conclusion; "and that finishes it."

Mr. Fox-Cordery's face lighted up.

"Long gray hair?" he asked.

"Yes," replied the hobbledehoy. "Could make a pair of wigs out of it."

"Down to here?" asked Mr. Fox-Cordery, with his hand at his breast.

"That's the wery identical. Looks like the Wizard of the North. Long legs and arms, face like a lion."

"That is the person I want," said Mr. Fox-Cordery.

"Third floor back," said the hobbledehoy; and, with the virtuous feeling of a boy who has earned his pennies, he walked into the house, with his head up; whereby Mr. Fox-Cordery learned that knockers and bells were superfluities, and that anyone was free of the street door, and could obtain entrance by a simple push. Following the instruction, he mounted the stairs slowly, lighting matches as he ascended to save himself from falling into a chance trap; a necessary precaution, for the passages were pitch dark, and the balustrades and staircases generally in a tumbledown, rickety condition. The third floor was the top of the house, and comprised one front and one back room. He knocked at the latter without eliciting a response, and knocked again with the same result. Then he turned the handle, which yielded to his pressure, and entered.

The room was as dark as the passages, and Mr. Fox-Cordery, after calling in vain, "Here, you, Rathbeal, you!" had recourse to his matchbox again; and seeing the end of a candle in a tall candlestick of curious shape upon the table, he lighted it and looked around. From the moment of his entering the room he had been conscious of a faint odor, rather disturbing to his senses, and now, as he looked around, he satisfied himself as to the cause. On a quaintly carved bracket were a bottle and a small box. The bottle was empty, but there was a little opium in the box.

"At his old game," he muttered. "Why doesn't it kill him? But I wouldn't have him die yet. I must first screw the truth out of him."

By "him" he meant the tenant of the room, who lay on a narrow bed asleep. Before disturbing him, Mr. Fox-Cordery devoted attention to the articles by which he was surrounded. The furniture of this humble attic was extraordinary of its kind, and had probably been picked up at odd times, in one auction-room and another. On the floor was an old Oriental rug, worn quite threadbare; the two chairs were antiques; the carved legs of the table represented the legs of fabulous animals; even the fire-irons were old-fashioned. There were several brackets on the walls, carved by the sleeping man, showing a quaint turn of fancy; and on each bracket rested an article of taste, here a small Eastern vase, here a twisted bottle, here the model of a serpent standing upright on two human legs. A dealer in old curiosities would not have given more than a sovereign or two for all the furniture and ornaments in the room, for none of them were of any particular value. But the collection was a remarkable one to be found in an attic in such a neighborhood; and, if it denoted nothing else, was an indication that the proprietor was not of the common order of English workingmen, such as one would have expected to occupy the apartment; if, indeed, he was an Englishman at all.

Mr. Fox-Cordery was not a gentleman of artistic taste, and he turned up his nose and shrugged his shoulders contemptuously at these belongings. Then he devoted a few moments more to an examination of the room, opening drawers without hesitation, and running his eyes over some manuscripts on the table. The written characters of these manuscripts were exquisite, albeit somewhat needlessly fantastic here and there: and the manuscripts themselves furnished a clew to the occupation of the tenant, which was that of a copyist. There were no paintings or engravings on the walls, which, however, were not entirely devoid of pictorial embellishment. Four neatly cut pieces of drawing-paper were tacked thereon—north, south, east, and west—bearing each a couplet beautifully written within an illuminated scroll. The colors of the scrolls were green and gold, and the verses were written in shining Indian ink.

On the tablet on the north wall the lines ran:

He whose soul by love is quickened, never can to death be hurled;
Written is my life immortal in the records of the world.

On the south wall:

Oh, heart! thy springtime has gone by, and at life's flowers has failed thy aim.
Gray-headed man, seek virtue now; gain honor and a spotless name.

On the west wall:

Now on the rose's palm the cup with limpid wine is brimming,
And with a hundred thousand tongues the bird her praise is hymning.

On the east wall:

If all upon the earth arise to injure myself or my friend,
The Lord, who redresses wrong, shall avenge us all in the end.

Mr. Fox-Cordery's judgment upon these couplets was that the writer's brain was softening; and considering that he had wasted sufficient time in making discoveries of no value, he stepped to the narrow bed, and contemplated the sleeper. The contrast between the two men was noteworthy, but it was the good or bad fortune of Mr. Fox-Cordery always to furnish a contrast of more or less interest when he stood side by side with his fellow-men. At this moment his clean, pallid face, with its carefully arranged hair and drooping mustache, wore an ugly expression singularly at odds with his diminutive stature.

It is not pleasant for a man with a thorough belief in his own supremacy to suspect that he has been tricked by one whom he gauges to be of meaner capacity than himself; but this had been Mr. Fox-Cordery's suspicion since his interview with John Dixon, and he had come hither either to verify or falsify it. The sleeper's age could not have been less than sixty years; he was a large-limbed man, six feet in height, and proportionately broad and massive. His full-fleshed eyelids with their shaggy eyebrows, his abundant tangled hair, and the noble gray beard descending to his breast, denoted a being of power and sensibility; and though he lay full length and unconscious beneath the little man who was gazing wrathfully upon him, he seemed to tower majestically above the pygmy form. Mr. Fox-Cordery shook the sleeper violently, and called:

"Rathbeal, you scoundrel; just you wake up! Do you hear? No shamming! Wake up!"

Rathbeal slowly opened his eyes, which like his hair were gray, and fixed them upon Mr. Fox-Cordery. Recognition of his unexpected visitor did not immediately come to him, and he continued to gaze in silence upon the intruder. Half asleep and half awake as he was, there was a magnetic quality in his eyes which did not tend to put Mr. Fox-Cordery at his ease; and in order to make a proper assertion of himself, he said, in a bullying tone:

"When you have had your stare out, perhaps you'll let me know."

The voice assisted Rathbeal, who, closing his eyes and with a subtle smile on his lips, murmured, in perfect English:

"The enemy thy secret sought to gain:

A hand unseen repelled the beast profane."

"Beast yourself!" retorted Mr. Fox-Cordery. "Here, no going off to sleep again! You're wanted, particularly wanted; and I don't intend to stand any of your infernal nonsense!"

But these lordly words, peremptorily uttered, did not seem to produce their intended effect, for Rathbeal, still with closed eyes, murmured:

"Be my deeds or good or evil, look thou to thyself alone;

All men, when their work is ended, reap the harvest they have sown."

The couplet, being of the order of those affixed to the walls, conveyed no definite idea, and certainly no satisfaction, to Mr. Fox-Cordery's mind. He cried masterfully:

"Are you going to get up or not? I've something to say to you; and you've got to hear it, if I stay all night."

Then Rathbeal opened his eyes again, and there was recognition in them, as he said courteously:

"Ah, Mr. Fox-Cordery, your pardon; I was scarcely awake. You have taken me from the land of dreams. It is the first time you have honored me in this apartment. To see you here is a surprise."

"I dare say," chuckled Mr. Fox-Cordery, "and not an agreeable one either. Eh, old man?"

"If it were not agreeable," said Rathbeal, spreading out his hands, which were large and shapely, and in keeping with his general appearance, "I should not confess it. You are my guest."

"Guest be hanged!" exclaimed Mr. Fox-Cordery, resenting the suggestion as claiming equality with him. "Do you think I have come to partake of your hospitality? Not by a long way. Are you awake yet?"

"Wide, very wide," replied Rathbeal, rising calmly from his bed. "I have been in the spirit"—he consulted a silver watch—"nine hours. If you had not aroused me I should have been by this time conscious. Excuse me; I have no other apartment." There was a small shut-up washstand in a corner, and he opened it, and pouring out water, laved his hands. When he had dried them he combed out his noble beard with his fingers, and said, "I am now ready for work."

"People, as a rule, leave off at this hour," remarked Mr. Fox-Cordery, who for reasons of his own, which had suggested themselves since he entered the room, did not intend to rush into his grievance. Under any circumstances he might not have done so, absorbing as it was, for it was his method to lead up to a subject artfully in the endeavor to gain some advantage beforehand.

"I commence at this hour," said Rathbeal, "and work through the night. You have something to say to me?"

"A good deal, and you'll need all your wits. I say, you, Rathbeal, what are you?" His eyes wandered about the room, and gave point to his inquiry. "I have known you a pretty long time, but I have never been able to make up my mind about you. Not that I have troubled myself particularly; but since I have been here I have grown curious. That's frank, isn't it?"

"Very. What am I? You open up a vast field. What is man? Who has been sufficiently wise to answer the question? What is man? What is life? Some say a dream, and that it commences with death. Some say that the soul of man exists long before the man is born, and that it is enshrined in a human body for the purpose of overcoming the temptations and debasing influences of the material life. Successful, it earns its place in celestial abodes, Unsuccessful, it is forever damned."

"You think yourself precious clever," sneered Mr. Fox-Cordery.

"No, I am an enigma to myself, as all reflective men must be."

"Reflective men!" exclaimed Mr. Fox-Cordery. "Hear him!"

"One thing I know," said Rathbeal, ignoring the taunt. "You, I, and all lesser and greater mortals, are part of a system."

"Hang your system, and your palaver with it! I'll tell you in a minute or two what I came here for, but I shall be obliged if you will first tell me something of yourself. I have the right to know your history."

"I have no objection. You wish to learn my personal history. It is soon told."

"None of your lies, you know; I shall spot them if you try to deceive me. I am as wide awake as you are."

"Wider, far wider. You have the wisdom of the serpent."

"Here, I say," cried Mr. Fox-Cordery, "none of your abuse. What do you mean by that?"

"You should receive it as a compliment." He pointed to the figure of a serpent on human legs standing on a bracket. "I compare you to the serpent in admiration. Shall I commence at the beginning of my life?"

"Commence where you like, only cut it short."

"My father was a Persian; my mother also. They came to England to save their lives. One week longer in Persia, and they would have been slain."

"A pity."

"That they did not remain in their native land? That they were not slain? Perhaps. Who shall say? But there is a fate. Who shall resist it? Safe in England, where I was born a week after their arrival, my parents lived till I was a youth. They imbued me with their spirit. As you see." He waved his hand around. "I live by the art of my pen. That is all."

"Quite enough; it is plain there is no getting anything out of you. Now, listen to me. You accepted a commission from me, which you led me to believe you fulfilled. If it is not fulfilled you practiced a fraud upon me for which the law can punish you."

"I am acquainted with the English law. I have a perception of a higher— the divine law. We will proceed fairly, for you have spoken of a serious business. Many years ago you desired some parchments copied, and, hearing I had some skill with the pen, you sought me out. I performed the work you intrusted to me, and from time to time you favored me with further orders. The engagement ended; you needed my pen no more. But you deemed me worthy to undertake a commission of another nature. You had a friend, or a foe, who was suffering, and whose presence in England was inconvenient to you."

"Lie number one," said Mr. Fox-Cordery.

"It is a true interpretation. You came to me and said, 'This man is dying; I wish his last hours to be peaceful. There are memories here that torture him. Make friends with him. Opium will relieve him; ardent spirits will assuage his pain; travel will beguile his senses. His constitution is broken. Go with him to Paris; I will allow you a small monthly stipend, and, when his pain is over, you shall have a certain sum for your labor.'"

"Lies, and lies, and yet more lies," said Mr. Fox-Cordery, watching Rathbeal's face warily. "You have a fine stock of them, and of all colors and shapes. Why, you would come out first in a competition."

"You compliment me," said Rathbeal, with a gentle smile. "Did those words exist only in my imagination? Yet, as you unfolded your wishes to me, halting and hesitating with a coward's reserve, I thought I heard them spoken. 'Do I know the unfortunate man?' I inquired, 'of whom you are so considerate, toward whom you are so mercifully inclined.' You replied that it was hardly likely, and you mentioned him by name. No, I had never heard of the gentleman. 'I must see him first,' I said, 'before giving you an answer.' You instructed me how to find him, and I sought him out, and made the acquaintance of a being racked with a mortal sorrow. You came to me the following day for an answer; I informed you that you had come too soon, and that I had not decided. 'Be speedy,' you urged. 'I am anxious to get the man out of my sight.'"

"Still another lie," said Mr. Fox-Cordery. "Not a word you have quoted was ever spoken by me."

"My imagination again," said Rathbeal, with the same gentle smile; "and yet they are in my mind. Perhaps I translated your thoughts as you went on. After a fortnight had passed I consented to your wishes, and your friend, or your foe, left England for the Continent in my company. It was expressly stipulated by you that no mention should be made by me of your goodness, and that if he asked for the name of the friend who was befriending him I was to answer guardedly that you wished to preserve it secret. Only once did he refer to you, and then not by name; but I understood him to say that he knew to whom he was indebted, and that there was only one man in the world who had not deserted him in his downfall."

"May I inquire," asked Mr. Fox-Cordery, "whether your companion let you into the secrets of his life—for we all have secrets, you know."

"Yes, every man, high and low. He did not; he preserved absolute silence respecting his history. We remained on the Continent a considerable time, supporting ourselves partly by your benefactions, partly by copying manuscripts, an art I taught him. I learned to love the gentleman to whom you had introduced me for some evil purpose of your own—"

"For an evil purpose! You are raving!"

"For some evil purpose of your own, which I could no more fathom than I could the nature of the sorrow that was consuming him. 'Try opium,' I said to him, 'it will help you to forget.' He refused. 'I will allow myself no indulgence.' And this, indeed, was true to the letter. He lived upon water and a bare crust. So did the monks of old, but their lives were less holy than his, for it was only of themselves and their own souls they thought, while he, with no concern for his own welfare, temporal or spiritual, thought only of others, and applied every leisure hour and every spare coin to their relief and consolation.

51

He was a singular mixture of qualities—"

"Spare me your moralizings," interrupted Mr. Fox-Cordery. "I knew what he was, long before you set eyes on him. Keep to the main road."

"In the life of every man," said Rathbeal, "though he be evil and corrupt, there are byways wherein flowers may be found, and it was of such byways I was about to speak in the life of this man of sorrow, who was neither evil nor corrupt; but I perceive you do not care to hear what I can say to his credit, so I will keep to the main road, as you bid me. There dwelt in my mind during all the time we spent in foreign lands the words you addressed to me: 'When you tell me that I shall be troubled with him no more, you will lighten my heart.'"

"How many more versions are you going to give," said Mr. Fox-Cordery, "of what I never said to you? You are a liar, self-confessed."

"Is that so? And yet, shrewd sir, I insist that the words are not of my sole coining. At length I was in a position to inform you that your desire was accomplished, and that your friend, or your foe, would trouble you no more; and so, upon my return to England—with the payment of a smaller sum than I expected from you, for you made deductions—all business between us came to an end. Upon your entrance into this room to-night I remarked that your presence was a surprise to me. I did not expect you, and I am puzzled to know how you discovered where I lodge."

"When I weave a web, Rathbeal," chuckled Mr. Fox-Cordery, "nothing ever escapes from it."

"An unfortunate figure of speech," said Rathbeal impressively, "for you liken yourself to a human spider. But there are other webs than those that mortals weave. Fate is ever at work; it is at work now, weaving a mesh for you, in spots invisible to you, in men and women who are strangers to you, and you shall no more escape from it than you shall escape from death when your allotted hour comes."

"Oh, I daresay. Go and frighten babies with your balderdash. What I have come to know is, whether you have obtained money from me under false pretenses. It is an offense for which the law provides—"

A movement on the part of his companion prevented him from finishing the sentence. Rathbeal had risen from his chair, and was standing by the door in the act of listening, and Mr. Fox-Cordery did not observe that he had slipped the key out of the lock. He was about to rise and throw open the door, in the hope of making a discovery which would bring confusion upon Rathbeal, when the latter, by a sudden and rapid movement, quitted the room. Mr. Fox-Cordery turned the handle of the door, with the intention of following him.

"Hanged if the beggar hasn't locked me in!" he cried, in consternation. "Here, you, Rathbeal, you! Play me any of your tricks, and I'll have the law of you! If you don't open the door this instant I'll call the police!"

No answer was made to the threat, and Mr. Fox-Cordery, seriously alarmed that he had fallen into a trap, and unable to open the door, though he shook it furiously, lifted the window-sash to call for help, but the room was at the back of the house, and when he put his head out of the window he could not pierce the dense darkness into which he peered. He screamed out nevertheless, and was answered by a touch upon his shoulder which caused him to tremble in every limb and to give utterance to a cry of fear. Turning, he saw Rathbeal smiling upon him.

"My shrewd sir," said Rathbeal, "what alarms you?"

Mr. Fox-Cordery recovered his courage instantly.

"Confound you!" he blustered. "What do you mean by locking me in?"

"Locking you in!" exclaimed Rathbeal, pointing to the key in the lock. "You are dreaming. I thought I heard a visitor ascending the stairs, and as I was sure you did not wish for the presence of a third party till our interview was over I went out to dismiss him."

"Or her," suggested Mr. Fox-Cordery, with malicious emphasis.

"Or her, if you will. Sit down and compose yourself. You were saying when I left the room that I had obtained money from you on false pretenses, and that it is an offense for which the law provides. It is doubtless the case— not that I have obtained your money falsely, but that the law could punish me if I had. Explain yourself. You came hither to speak to me, and yet it is I who have chiefly spoken. You have heard me; let me hear you."

"What I want to know," said Mr. Fox-Cordery, "and what I will know, is whether you have given me false information."

"Upon what subject, shrewd sir?"

"Upon the subject you have been speaking of."

"You must be more explicit. If I choose not to admit that I understand you when you speak in vague terms it is because of the attitude you have assumed toward me, which you will excuse me for remarking is deficient in politeness. Speak clearly, shrewd sir, and you shall have like for like. I will not be behindhand with you in frankness."

"All right. I wished to serve a friend who was in a bad way. He was broken down, and needed change of air and scene; I provided the means, and sent you with him as a companion who might have a beneficial effect upon him. I did not expect him to recover; he was too far gone-his health being completely shattered. As a matter of course I did not wish the thing to go on forever, and I desired to be kept posted how it progressed, and, if it came to the worst, to be informed at the earliest moment. You informed me that all was over, that my poor friend was dead, and I paid you handsomely for your personal attention to the matter. Am I to understand that the information you gave me was true?"

"I pin you to greater clearness, shrewd sir, or you will obtain no answer from me."

"The devil seize you! Is it true that the man I speak of is dead?"

"Did I so inform you?"

"You did."

"I have no recollection of it. You have my letter. Produce it. The written words are—I can recall them—'Rest content. Your desire is compassed; you will be troubled no more.' Pay a little attention now to me, shrewd sir. You have spoken to me in unmannerly fashion; you have threatened me with the law. I despise your threats; I despise you. Profit by a lesson it will be well for you to learn in this humble room. Never make an enemy of a man, not even of the meanest man. You never know when he may help to strike you down. When I worked for you as a copyist you formed an estimate of my character upon grounds shaped by yourself for your own private purposes—purposes into which, up to the present moment, I have made no active inquiry, though I have pondered upon them. I do not engage myself to be in the future so practically incurious and retiring."

"Bully away," said Mr. Fox-Cordery, inwardly boiling over with rage. "I have nothing to fear from you."

"You said to yourself, 'Here is a man of foreign origin who will do anything for money,' and this opinion emboldened you to proceed with a scheme which needed an unscrupulous agent, such as you supposed me to be, to insure success. Unsolicited you introduced your scheme to me, not in plain words, for which you could be made directly accountable, but in veiled allusions and metaphors which needed intellectual power to comprehend. Intellect is required for the success of base as well as of worthy ends. Your mock compassion amazed me, and I made a mental study of you, as of something new—a confession which perhaps will surprise you. Not I the dupe, shrewd sir, but you. Men of my nation have a habit of expressing themselves in metaphor, and are taught to grasp a meaning, not from what is said, but from what is not said; and I, though I have never been in my parents' native land, acquired this habit from them. I divined your wish, but saw not, and see not now, the springs which prompted it. Plainly, it was a crime you proposed to me, and left the means at my discretion; and after making the acquaintance of the gentleman whose end you hired me to compass, I accepted the commission, nothing being farther from my mind than to assist in its accomplishment. Not I, but fortune, favored you. You were troubled by a mortal's existence; you were released from your trouble, and your end was attained. Thus much I tell you, and will tell you no more. Be content, and go."

"Come now," said Mr. Fox-Cordery, drawing a long breath of relief, "you have talked a lot of infernal bosh, and told any number of lies; but I will excuse you for everything if you will inform me where it took place."

"Not one word will I add to those I have already spoken."

"Hang it! I have a right to know. You could be forced to tell!"

"Make the attempt. For the second time, I bid you go."

He threw open the door, and stood aside to give his visitor unobstructed passage. Recognizing the uselessness of remaining any longer, Mr. Fox-Cordery laughed insolently in Rathbeal's face, and, feeling his way down the dark stairs, reached the lower landing in safety, and passed into the street.

Although he was not in the most amiable of humors, his mind was greatly relieved. Robert Grantham was dead. Of that he had been assured by Rathbeal; not, certainly, in such plain words as he would have preferred to hear, but in terms that left no doubt in his mind.

"I put his back up," he muttered, as he walked along, "and that is why he wouldn't speak out. Besides, he wasn't going to criminate himself. I was an idiot to take the trouble I did over the affair. Grantham was quite broken down at the time, and couldn't have lasted long under any circumstances. There isn't an office in England that would have taken a year's insurance on his life. He was done for; death was in his face. They have all played into my hands, every one of them."

But notwithstanding the relief he experienced, the events of the day were not of a nature to afford him pleasant reflection. He had been three times defied. First by Charlotte, then by John Dixon, then by Rathbeal. Charlotte he did not fear as an enemy; despite her outbreak, he had been too long accustomed to dominate her to be apprehensive of her. She was in his power, and had pledged herself to silence for two months. John Dixon and Rathbeal stood on a different platform; but even from them he had little if anything to fear. As to John Dixon's account of having seen Robert Grantham's face in a fog, he snapped his fingers at it. It was, at best, a clumsy invention; had he been in Dixon's place, he would have done better. His enemies had put him on his guard—that was all the good they had done for themselves.

When he reached the middle of Westminster Bridge, he paused and looked down into the water. The darkness had lifted a little, and a few stars had come out and were reflected in the river. The lamps upon the banks formed a long line of restless, shifting light, converging to a point in the far distance. An imaginative mind could have woven rare fancies out of the glimmering sheen in the river's heart, which seemed to pulse with spiritual life. Cathedral aisles, with dusky processions winding between, descending into the depths to make room for those that crowded behind. Lights upon a distant battlefield, a confused tangle of horses and fighting men, the wounded and dying crawling into the deep shades. A wash of the waves, and a wild _mèlée_ of dancers was created, lasting but a moment—as, indeed, did all the pictures,—and separating into peaceable units with the broadening out of the water. A ripple, almost musical in its poetic silence, bearing bride and bridegroom to love and joy. A band of rioters, upheaving, with waving limbs inextricably mingled, replaced by an orderly line of hooded monks, gliding on with folded arms.

None of these pictures presented themselves to Mr. Fox-Cordery's imagination. He saw only two figures in the water: one of a dead man floating onward to oblivion; the other of a woman with peaceful, shining face, inviting him, with smiling eyes, to come to her embrace. The wish was father to the thought, and the figures were there as he had conjured them up. The face of the dead man brought no remorse to his soul; he was susceptible only of those affections in which his own personal safety and his own personal desires were concerned. It was for the death of this man and the possession of this woman that he had schemed and toiled. The man he hated, and had pursued to his ruin; the woman he loved and would have bartered his soul for. His passion for her had grown to such a pitch as to make him reckless of consequences; or, more properly speaking, blind to them. Had she yielded to his wooing in years gone by, he would have made a slave of her, and have tyrannized over her as he did over all with whom he had dealings. But she had not favored him, except in the way of friendship, and had given herself to the man he hated and despised. It can scarcely be said that a nature so mean and cruel as his was capable of pure and honest love; but passion and baffled desire took the place of love, and had obtained such complete possession of his senses that he was not master of himself where she was concerned. At his age the fever of the blood should have been cooled, but opposition and disappointment had produced a kind of frenzy in him; and, in addition, he had always been a law unto himself, ready to put his foot upon the neck of any living creature who ventured to obstruct his lightest wish.

A black cloud blotted out the stars; the beautiful face disappeared. Awaking from his reverie, Mr. Fox-Cordery proceeded to cross the bridge. Staggering toward him in the opposite direction was a lad in the last stage of want and destitution; a large-eyed, white-faced lad literally clothed in rags. His trousers were held up by a piece of knotted string, crossing his breast and back; he had no cap on his matted hair; his naked toes peeped out of his boots. That he was faint and ill was evident from his staggering gait, and indeed he hardly knew where he was going, so genuinely desperate was his forlorn condition. It chanced that he stumbled against the dapper form of Mr. Fox-Cordery, who, crying, "What's your game, you young ruffian?" gave him a brutal push, and sent him reeling into the road. The lad had no strength to save himself from falling. Gasping for breath, he clutched at the air, and fell, spinning, upon the stones. Passing callously on, Mr. Fox-Cordery did not observe, and was not observed by a man who, seeing the lad fall, ran forward to assist him. Stooping and raising the lad's head, the man looked into his face.

"Why, Billy!" cried the man compassionately.

The lad opened his eyes, smiled faintly, and answered, "Yes, it's me, Mr. Gran "; and then the dark clouds seemed to fall upon him, and he lay limp and insensible in the man's arms.

CHAPTER VII.

Billy turns the Corner.

Robert Grantham for a moment was undecided what to do. No one was near them; he and Billy were just then alone on the bridge. Resolving upon his course of action, he raised Billy in his arms and walked with his burden toward Rathbeal's lodging. Billy was nothing of a weight for a man to carry, being but skin and bone, and Grantham experienced no difficulty in the execution of the merciful task he had taken upon himself. He was not troubled by inquiries from the few persons he encountered. A policeman looked after them, but as Grantham made no appeal to him, and there was no evidence of the law being broken, he turned and resumed his beat. Robert Grantham was a quarter of an hour walking to the house in which Rathbeal lodged. Without hesitating, he pushed the street door open, and ascended the stairs. Rathbeal heard him coming up, and waited for him on the landing.

"What have you got there?" he asked.

"A lump of misery," replied Grantham.

Rathbeal made way for his friend, who entered the room and laid Billy on the bed. Then he examined the lad to see if any bones were broken, Rathbeal, better skilled than he, assisting him.

"Where did you find him, Robert?"

"On Westminster Bridge. He must have stumbled against someone who pushed him off into the road, where he fell fainting. I have known the poor little fellow for months, but I have not seen him for the last three or four weeks. I wondered what had become of him."

"Where do his people live?"

"Heaven knows! He has none, I believe; or at all events, none who care to look after him. He is a waif of the streets, not an uncommon growth in London."

"You have been good to him?"

"I have given him bread sometimes, when I had it to give; and the last time I met him I took him home with me, and made up a bed on the floor for him. He remained with me a week, and then he unaccountably disappeared. What is to be done? He does not recover. He is not dead, thank God! There is a faint beat of the heart."

Rathbeal produced a bottle in which there was some brandy. He moistened the lad's lips with the spirit, and poured a few drops, diluted with water, down his throat. Still the lad did not open his eyes.

"Have you anything to eat in the cupboard?" asked Robert Grantham.

"There is a little bread and meat," said Rathbeal.

"He looks scarcely strong enough to be able to masticate hard food. Make some water hot, Rathbeal. I will go and get a packet of oatmeal; a basin of gruel will be the best thing for him."

"Wait a minute, Robert." Rathbeal devoted a few moments to the lad, and added gravely: "On the opposite side of the road, half a dozen doors down, there is a poor man's doctor. Ask him to come up at once and see the boy."

"I will;" and meeting Rathbeal's eyes, he said, "Do you fear there is any danger?"

"Yes. I have some medical skill, as you know; but I do not hold a diploma. It will be advisable that a doctor should see the poor boy."

Robert Grantham nodded, and took from his pocket all the money it contained—one sixpence and a few coppers. Rathbeal handed him five shillings.

"Thank you, Rathbeal," said Grantham, and ran down the stairs. In less than ten minutes he was back, with a packet of oatmeal, and accompanied by the doctor. While the doctor examined the lad, Rathbeal busied himself in the preparation of the gruel, the kettle, already nearly boiling, standing on a little gas-stove.

"Yes," said the doctor, noticing the preparation; "it will be the proper food to give him when he comes to his senses. Put a teaspoonful of brandy in it. A son of yours?"

"No," answered Grantham; "my friend, Mr. Rathbeal, has never seen him before. I found him in this condition in the street."

"Where are his parents?"

"I do not know, nor whether he has any."

"But you must have had some previous knowledge of him," said the doctor, looking with curiosity at Grantham.

"Oh, yes. I met him by chance some months since, when he was in want of food, and we struck up an acquaintance. Is he in danger?"

"He may not live through the night." He put up his hand; Billy was coughing, and a little pink foam gathered about his lips, which the doctor wiped away. "Exposure and want have reduced him to this state. He has been suffering a long time, and his strength is completely wasted. Had he been attended to months ago, there would have been a chance for him. Listen!" Billy was coughing again, a faint, wasting cough, painful to hear. "I can do very little. I will send you a bottle of medicine, which may give him temporary relief; and I will come again about midnight, if you wish."

"I shall feel obliged to you. We shall be here all night. Should he have brandy after he has taken the gruel?"

"A few drops now and then will do him no harm. He needs all the strength you can put into him. Endeavor to get from him some information about his relatives, and go for them."

"Would it be best to take him to a hospital?"

"He should not be removed; he will not trouble you long."

"It is mo... grief than a trouble."

"I understand. See, he is coming to. How do you feel now, my little man?"

"_I_ do... know," murmured Billy. "There's somethink 'ere." He moved his hand feebly to his chest. "Is that you, Mr. Gran? Where am I?"

"With good friends, Billy."

"You've allus been that to me, sir."

"Now try and eat a little of this," said Grantham, raising the lad gently in his arms.

B...y, with a grateful smile, managed to get two or three spoonfuls down, and ...en... back on the bed.

"Do 't orce im," said the doctor. "Where do you live, Billy?"

"I don't kn... —anywhere."

"But try an... emember."

"I can't 'member nothink—only Mr. Gran. It ain't likely I'll forgit 'im. Thank yer kindly, sir, for wot you've done for me; there ain't many like yer."

He closed his eyes, and appeared to sleep.

"I will see hi... g in at midnight," said the doctor, and stepped softly from the room.

Rathbeal cleared the table, and arranged some manuscripts.

"We may as well work while we watch, Robert. These must be copied by the morning."

He spoke in a whisper, and, sitting down, commenced to write. Grantham lingered awhile by the bedside, and as Billy did not stir, presently joined his friend, and proceeded with his copying. He did not observe that Billy, when he left his side, slyly opened his eyes, and gazed upon him with a look of grateful, pathetic love. Every time Grantham turned to him he closed his eyes, in order that it should be supposed he was sleeping. The writing proceeded almost in silence, the friends only exchanging brief, necessary words relating to their work. Now and then Grantham rose and went to the bedside, and when the bottle of medicine arrived he laid his hand gently on Billy's shoulder.

"Yes, Mr. Gran," said the lad, "I'm awake."

"Take this, Billy; it will do you good."

"Nothink'll do me good, sir; but I'll take it. I _did_ want to see you before

I went where I'm going to."

"There, there, my dear boy," said Robert Grantham, "you must not exhaust yourself by talking too much. You have taken the medicine bravely. Now try and swallow a spoonful of gruel."

He had kept it hot for the lad on the gas-stove.

"Thank you, Mr. Gran, I'll try; but I _should_ like to know where I'm going to."

"If you do not get well, Billy, you will be in a better place than this."

"Glad to 'ear it, sir; though luck's agin me. Yer didn't think it bad o' me to cut away from yer so sly, did yer?"

"No, my lad, no; but what made you go?"

"I'll tell yer 'ow it was, sir. I didn't want to take the bread out of yer mouth, and I found out I was doing it, without yer ever saying a word about it. There was the last day I was with yer, Mr. Gran; you 'ad dry bread, I 'ad treacle on mine; yer give me a cup 'o broth, and water was good enough for you. At supper you didn't take a bite of anythink, while I was tucking away like one o'clock. 'It's time for you to cut yer lucky, Billy,' I sed; and I did."

"Foolish lad! foolish lad!" said Robert Grantham, smoothing Billy's hair. "Where did you go to?"

"I don' know, Mr. Gran—into the country somewhere; but I didn't 'ave better luck there than 'ere, sir. I was took bad, and I was told I was dying; but I got better, Mr. Gran, and strong enough to walk back to London. I only come to-night, sir. When I was bad in the country, an old woman sed I was done for, and that if I didn't pray for salvation I should go to—you know where, sir. She give me a ha'penny, and sed, 'Now, you go away and pray as 'ard as yer can.' But I didn't think that'd do me any good, and ses I to myself, 'I'll toss up for it. Heads, salwation; tails, t'other.' I sent the ha'penny spinning, and down it come—tails, t'other. Jest like my luck, wasn't it, Mr. Gran?"

"Billy," said Robert Grantham earnestly, "you must drive that notion out of your head. We are all equal in the sight of God—"

"Oh, are we, Mr. Gran? That's a 'ard notion, as yer call it, to drive out o' my head, and I don't think I've got time for it. Beggin' yer pardon, sir."

Rathbeal, pen in hand, stopped in his work, and listened to the conversation.

"I tell you we are all equal in the eyes of God—rich and poor, high and low. The prayers of a poor boy reach God's ears as readily as the prayers of a rich man."

"If _you_ prayed, Mr. Gran," said Billy, "Gawd'd listen to yer. Per'aps yer wouldn't mind praying for me a bit."

Robert Grantham covered his eyes with his hand.

"'Ave I 'urt yer, sir?" moaned Billy. "Don't say I've 'urt yer!"

"No, my boy, no. If I had as little to answer for as you—" He paused awhile. "Your state is not of your own creating, Billy."

"No, sir; I don't know as it is. I couldn't 'elp bein' wot I am."

"There are many who could not say as much, who walk into sin with their eyes wide open—Billy!"

The lad was seized with a sudden paroxysm of coughing, which lasted several minutes. The fit over, he lay back exhausted, the red foam issuing from his mouth. It was no time for exhortation. Robert Grantham cleared the fatal sign from the sufferer's mouth, and patted Billy's hand and stroked his face pitifully. Billy's lips touched the consoling hand.

"Thank yer, sir. Let me lay still a bit."

The men resumed their work, and the boy was quiet. At midnight the doctor called again.

"As I feared," he said, apart to Robert Grantham; "he will last but a few hours."

Robert Grantham asked him what his fee was. The doctor shook his head, and said:

"I have done nothing; I could do nothing. Permit me to play my humble part in your kind charity. Good-night."

He shook hands with them, put Billy in an easy position, and left them.

"It isn't altogether a bad world, Robert," observed Rathbeal.

"It is what we make it," replied Robert Grantham, with a heavy sigh.

"That will not apply to the poor outcast lying there," said Rathbeal, looking at Billy.

"True, true," rejoined Grantham. "I was thinking of my own life."

Rathbeal had the intention, when Mr. Fox-Cordery left him, of saying something about his visit, but this sad adventure had put it out of his head. He thought of his intention now, when Robert Grantham said the world was what we made it; and he resolved that before many days had passed he would invite his friend's confidence in a direct way. In the presence of death he could not do so, and he set the matter aside for the present.

Their copying was finished at three o'clock, and Rathbeal gathered the pages, and put them in order. There had been no apparent change in the lad, but the solemnity of the scene impressed the men deeply. The house was very quiet, and no sound came to them from the street. They had endeavored, without success, to obtain from Billy some information of his relations. Either he did not or would not understand them, for he gave them no intelligible replies to their questions. They decided to make another effort during the next interval of consciousness, and, sitting by his bedside, they watched their opportunity. It came as Rathbeal's watch pointed to the hour of four. Billy raised his lids; his hands moved feebly. The men inclined their ears. Rathbeal left it to Robert Grantham to speak.

"Billy!"

"Yes, Mr. Gran; yes, sir."

"I want you, for my sake, to try and remember. You had a father and mother?"

"Yes, Mr. Gran, a long time ago."

"Where are they?"

"I don' know, sir."

"Is it very long since you saw them?"

"Oh, ever so long!"

"But there must be someone—an aunt or uncle."

"Nobody, nobody!"

"Try, Billy; try to recollect—for my sake, remember."

"Yes, sir; yes, Mr. Gran, I'll try."

But he seemed to forget it immediately, for he said nothing more.

It must have been half-an-hour after this that Rathbeal touched Robert Grantham's arm impressively. The dews of death were on Billy's forehead, and his lips were moving.

"Prue, little Prue!" he murmured.

"A girl's pet name, probably," whispered Rathbeal in Robert Grantham's ear.

"Yes, Billy, yes," prompted Grantham; "who is little Prue?"

"Sweethearts we wos. Little Prue! little Prue!"

At this dying boy's mouth Fate was weaving its web; and some miles away Mr. Fox-Cordery was dreaming of the woman he loved and the friend he had ruined.

"Where does she live, Billy?"

"We wos sweethearts. I liked little Prue."

"Try and remember where she lives, Billy."

"Is that you speaking, Mr. Gran?"

"Yes, my boy. Do you understand what I say?"

"I don' know. 'Now you go away and pray as 'ard as ever yer can,' the old woman ses, and I goes away and tosses up for it. 'Eads, salwation; tails, t'other. And down it comes—tails. Just like my luck. But there's something I _do_ want to pray for! It's all I can do for 'im, and he ses Gawd'll 'ear a pore boy. So 'ere goes. Where's my ha'penny to toss with? No, I don't mean that. I mean Gawd, are yer listenin'?"

"Say your prayer, Billy," whispered Grantham, seeing that the lad's last moments had come; "God is listening to you."

"O Lawd Gawd!" prayed Billy, pausing painfully between each word; "give Mr. Gran all he wants, and a bit over. Look out! I am going to turn the corner."

A few moments afterward Billy had turned the corner, and was traveling on the road of Eternity, with angels smiling on him.

CHAPTER VIII.

The Gambler's Confession.

"You have asked me two or three times lately, my dear Rathbeal," wrote Robert Grantham, "to relate to you the story of my life, and you have mysteriously hinted that it might be in your power to render me a valuable

64

service, and perhaps to restore the happiness which it was evident to you I had lost. I did not respond to your friendly advances, in which there was a note of affection which touched me deeply; but it seems to me now churlish to refuse the confidence you ask for. It was not because I doubt you that I remained silent. I have long known that I possess in you a friend whose feelings for me are truly sincere, and who would be only too willing to make any personal sacrifice in his power to console and comfort me in my misery. That, indeed, you have already done; and although I can never repay the debt of gratitude I owe you, rest assured, dear friend, that I am deeply sensible of your sympathetic offices. But you can go no farther than this. All your wisdom and goodness would not avail to fulfill the hopes you entertain for my future. So far as I am personally and selfishly concerned I have no earthly future. I shaped my course, and marched straight on—deaf to the dictates of conscience, blind to virtue and suffering—so steeped in the vice that enslaved me, that it was only when the fell destroyer Death took from me the treasures which should have been my redemption, that the consciousness of my wrong-doing rushed upon me, and stabbed me to the heart. It was then too late for repentance, too late to fall upon my knees and pray for mercy and forgiveness. I deserved my punishment, and I bowed my head to it, not with meekness and resignation, but with a bitterness and scorn for myself which words are powerless to portray.

"I cannot recall when it was that I first became a gamester, but it was during my school-days that my evil genius obtained a mastery over me that I did not shake off until it had compassed my ruin and the ruin of innocent beings I should have cherished and protected. In the school I went to I had a friend and comrade, a lad of amiable parts and qualities, with whom I chiefly associated; and somehow it happened that he and I fell into the habit of playing cards for our pocket-money. I was not even then a fortunate player, but the loss of my few shillings was amply repaid by the delight I took in these games of chance. There were occasions when my friend reproved me for my infatuation, but I would not listen to him, and I made it a point of honor with him that he should give me opportunities of regaining the money I had lost. Not that I had any great desire to win my money back; it was play I craved for. He was much more concerned at my losses than myself; and I remember once that he offered to return all he had won, which, of course, I would not listen to.

"When, school-days over, I commenced to live the life of a man, I sought places and opportunities for pursuing my favorite pastime. I became a member of private clubs established for the gratification of enthusiasts like myself, and there I lost my money and enjoyed myself to my heart's content. I never questioned myself as to the morality of my passion, and whether I won or lost was almost a matter of indifference to me, so far as the actual value of the money I left behind me, or took away with me, was concerned. I had ample means, for more than one fortune was bequeathed to me; and I continued on the fatal road I had entered with so much zeal, and never once thought of turning back. At this period of my life the vice harmed no one but myself. If it had, I might have reflected; but how dare I make this lame excuse for my sinful conduct when I know that in after times it did affect others, and that even then I did not turn back?

"My friendship and intimacy with my schoolmate continued, and he often accompanied me to my favorite haunts, and gambled a little, but not to the same extent as I did, and with better luck. He accompanied me to France and Italy, where I found ample scope for indulgence in my besetting vice. By this time my schoolmate and I were bosom friends and inseparable; and when he remonstrated with me on my last night's losses, I used to laugh at him, and to challenge him there and then to sit down with me to a game of chance, saying, 'Someone must win my money, why not you?' And our intimacy was of such a nature that he could not refuse, though his compliance was not too readily given. At the Continental gaming-tables he would be my banker when I was cleaned out, and one day he suggested that he should act as a kind of steward of my fortune, which was still considerable. I consented gladly enough, for I had no head for figures, and he saved me a world of trouble. Then something took place which ought to have saved me, had not my besetting vice taken such absolute possession of me as to deprive me completely of moral control. I met a young and beautiful girl, and fell in love with her. My love was returned, and in a few months afterward she became my wife.

"Surely that should have opened my eyes to my folly, if anything could. A sweet and pure influence was by my side; and it is true that for a little while my mad course was checked. I was happy in my wife's society, as no man could fail to be who enjoyed the heaven of her love. A sweeter, nobler lady never drew breath. I tremble with shame as I write of her; I shudder with remorse as I think of the fate to which I brought her. For we had not been married many months before my evil genius began to haunt and tempt me. Understand that I should not then have spoken of my vice as an evil genius. I saw no evil in it, and I thought I had a right to pursue my pleasure; and so I began gradually to neglect my home, and to resume my old pursuit.

"My angel wife did not complain; she bore my neglect with sweetness and patience—smiling upon me when I left her side, smiling upon me when I returned. She had no knowledge of my secret; she did not see her fatal rival at my elbow wooing me away from her pure companionship. Some unrecognized feeling of shame kept me from exposing my degrading weakness to her. She devoted herself to her child, and by a thousand innocent arts—they make my heart bleed as I think of them—strove to win me more constantly to her side.

"Yes, Rathbeal, we had a child, a sweet flower from heaven, whose grace and beauty should have opened my eyes to my sin. Do not think that I did not love them. When I was with them, when I held my sweet little girl on my lap and felt her little hands upon my face, I thanked God for giving me a treasure so lovely and fair. Then my wife would timidly ask me whether I would not remain at home that night, and my evil genius would tempt me so sorely that I had not the strength to resist. It is a shameful confession, but having commenced I will go through with it to the bitter end; and if it lose me your friendship, if you turn from me in scorn for my folly and weakness, I must accept it as a part of my punishment.

"My angel wife suffered, and her sufferings increased as time went on. I did not see it then; I do now. She grew thin and pale, believing that I no longer loved her, believing that I repented my union with her. What else could she believe as she saw the ties of home weakening day by day? There are women who, in such a strait, would have challenged the man boldly, but she was not one of these. Her nature was too pliant and gentle, and terrible must have been her grief as she felt the rock she depended upon for protection and support crumbling away at her touch.

"My luck never varied. Occasionally, it is true, I won small sums, but these were invariably counterbalanced shortly afterward by heavier losses. The consequence was that the inroads upon my fortune became too serious to be overlooked. I asked my friend and steward for a large sum of money to pay a gambling debt; he looked grave. I inquired why he was so serious, and he invited me to look over the accounts. I did so; and though I could not understand the array of figures he placed before me, I saw clearly that my large fortune was almost entirely gone.

"'I have warned you,' said my friend, 'time after time; I could do no more.'

"'Spare me your reproaches,' I said. 'You have been a good friend, and I have paid no heed to your warnings. Wind up my affairs, and tell me how much I have left.'

"The following day he informed me that I still had three thousand pounds I could call my own.

"'Would you like a check for it?' he asked.

"I answered, 'Yes,' and he gave it to me.

"'And here,' he said, 'my stewardship ends. You must give me a full quittance of all accounts between us.'

"I drew up the paper at his dictation. He preferred, he said, that the quittance should be in my own handwriting; and when he had done I added words of thanks for the services he had rendered me, and signed the document.

"That night he accompanied me to a club, and watched my play. I won five hundred pounds, and we walked away together, late in the morning, in the highest spirits. He parted from me at the door of my house.

"'Will you play to-morrow night?' he asked.

"'Of course I shall play to-morrow night,' I replied, 'and every night after that. I will get back every shilling I have lost. Look at what I have done already; I have won five hundred pounds.'

"'It is your only chance of saving your wife and child from beggary,' he said.

"I thought of his words as I stepped softly into the house: 'My only chance of saving my wife and child from beggary.' It was true. It was a duty I owed to them to continue to play and win back the fortune I had lost. It was not my money; it was theirs. I was their only dependence. Yes, they should not say in the future that I had ruined their lives. Luck must change; it had commenced to smile upon me. There entered into my soul that night, Rathbeal, the spirit of greed. I had been too careless hitherto, too unmindful as to whether I won or lost. Hereafter I would be more careful; I would be cunning, as the men I played with were. I would invent a system which would break them and every man I played with. Tired as I was, I sat down and began to calculate chances. A newspaper was on the table, and when I had jotted down some columns of figures, and, aided by my recollection of certain bets I had made a night or two before, proved that had I played wisely I ought to have won instead of lost, I took up the newspaper, and carelessly ran my eyes down its columns. They stopped at an account of an Englishman's marvelous winnings at Monte Carlo—forty thousand pounds in three days. I pondered over it. If he, why not I? I would go and get my money back there. Sometimes in the haunts I frequented money ran short; men, winning, would leave with their gains, and there was no one left to play with except the losers, and I knew from experience how desperate that chance was. At Monte Carlo there was unlimited money. You could continue playing as long as you liked, and go away with your winnings in your pockets in hard cash. Witness this Englishman with his forty thousand pounds in three days. But it would be as well to take a large sum of money with me. I had over three thousand pounds;

I would make it into ten here, and then would go to Monte Carlo to wrest back my fortune. My mind made up, I crept to my bedroom. My wife was there, sleeping as I thought. In an adjoining room slept my little girl, Clair. Standing at the bedside of my wife I observed—shame upon me! for the first time with any consciousness that I was the cause of the change—how white and thin she had become. The sight of her wan face, and of her lovely lashes still moist with the tears she had shed, cut me like a knife. I did not dare to kiss her; I feared that she would awake and see my face, for I had looked at it in the glass, and was shocked at my haggard appearance. I stepped softly into the adjoining room where our little Clair was sleeping. She was rosy with health and young life, her red lips parted, showing her pearly teeth, her hair in clustering curls about her brow. Her I did not fear that I should awake, her slumbers were so profound, and I stooped and kissed her.

"'Robert!' said my wife.

"She had been awake when I entered her room, but had not opened her eyes lest she should offend me. Hearing me go into our child's bedroom, she had risen quietly and followed me.

"'Lucy!' I replied, my hands upon her shoulders.

"She fell into my arms, weeping, but no sound escaped her. Clair slept and must not be disturbed.

"I drew her into our bedroom, and closed the door upon Clair.

"'What is the matter, Lucy?' I asked. 'Are you not well?'

"She lifted her wet eyes with a sad wonder in them.

"'Did you not know, Robert?'

"'Know! What?'

"'That the doctor has been attending me lately,' she answered. 'Do not let it trouble you, dear. You also are not well. How changed you are! how changed! There is something on your mind, my dear."

"She did not say this in reproach, but in loving entreaty and pity; and though she did not directly ask me to confide in her, I understood her appeal. But I did not dare to confess my folly and my shame. I had kept my secret well, and she did not suspect it. No, I would not expose my degradation to her and my child. Perhaps, when I had won back the fortune I had lost, when I could say, 'I have not completely ruined your future,' then I might find courage to tell her all. But now, when I was nearly beggared and fortune was in my grasp, I must be silent; my secret must be kept from her.

"'It is nothing, Lucy,' I said; 'nothing. What does the doctor say?'

"She withdrew from my embrace, and said, coldly I thought:

"'I am not very well; that is all, Robert.'

"Nothing more passed between us that night. I believed—because I wished to believe—that there was nothing serious the matter with her; and if I was right in my conjecture that she was cold to me, it sprang probably because I would not confess what was weighing on my mind.

"How shall I describe the events of the next few weeks? Night after night I went from my home and kept out, often till daylight, endeavoring to wrest my losses from my fellow-gamesters. My wife did not ask me now to remain with her; she did not complain, and no further reference was made to the doctor. This was a comfort to me. If there had been anything to be really alarmed at I should not have been kept in ignorance of it. So I went blindly on, greedy now for money, chafing at my losses, suspecting all around me, and yet continuing to play till I had completely beggared myself. My companions did not know. It was not likely I was going to confess to them that if I lost I had not the means of paying. They continued to play with me, and I got in their debt, inventing excuses for being short of money. It was only temporary, I said; I should be in funds very soon. Do you see, Rathbeal, how low I had fallen?

"A sharper experience was to be mine. I lost a large sum and my paper was out for two thousand pounds. It was a debt of honor and must be paid. The misery of it was that I had perfected a system at roulette, which, with money at my command, could not possibly fail; and I had no means at my disposal to go to Monte Carlo, where unlimited wealth was awaiting me. It would be necessary to break up my home, but even that would not supply me with sufficient funds to pay my debts of honor and go to Monte Carlo. There was but one course open to me. My wife had a small private fortune of her own; I would ask her to advance me a portion of it as a loan which I would soon repay. I broached the subject to her.

"'It is only temporary,' I said, annoyed with myself that they should be the same words I had used to the men who held my paper.

"'You know how much I have, Robert,' she said, averting her eyes from me. 'It is Clair's more than mine. She must not be left penniless. I do not think you ought to ask me for so large a sum.'

"I mentioned a lower sum, and she said:

"'Yes, Robert, you can have that. Do not ask me for more.'

"I felt humiliated at this bargaining, and angry with her for her coldness and want of sympathy with me. I summoned up a false courage, and said it was likely that I should have to break up our home. She expressed no surprise.

"'In a little while, Lucy,' I said,' I will provide you with a better.'

"She did not wish for a better, she said; she could be happy in the humblest cottage, if— And then she paused and sighed, and I saw the tears in her eyes. I took her hand; she gently withdrew it.

"'I intended to tell you something to-day,' she said. 'My health has broken down. The doctor says I must leave England as soon as possible if I wish to live. I do wish to live, for my dear Clair's sake.'

"'Not for mine, Lucy?'

"I saw a struggle going on within her, but she sighed heavily again, and did not reply.

"'I am grieved to hear the doctor's report,' I said. 'May he not be mistaken?'

"'He is not mistaken. If I remain here I shall die.'

"'Where does he tell you to go to?'

"'To some village in the south of France, near the sea, where there is perfect quiet, where there are few people and no excitement.'

"Such a place, I thought, would be death to me, with the plan I had in my head of my projected venture at Monte Carlo.

"'Very well, Lucy,' I said; 'if it must be, it must be. I will join you there.'

"'You cannot go with us?'

"'Not immediately. I have something of the utmost importance to attend to elsewhere. It will not occupy me long, and then I will come to you.'

"'I did not expect you would accompany us,' she said.

"Not once had she looked at me or turned toward me. The impression her conduct made upon me was not so strong then as afterward, when I awoke from my dream of wealth, and when Fate dealt me the fatal stroke.

"We parted. I received the money I asked her to lend me from her little fortune, and we parted. I stood on the platform with her and our Clair; my faithful friend and once steward stood a little apart from us. He had offered to go with them to Dover, and his services had been accepted. It was impossible for me to go even so far. My creditors were clamoring, and I had arranged to meet a broker at my house, to sell him everything in it, and to get the money immediately from him. If my debts of honor were not paid that evening, I was threatened with public exposure. Therefore it was imperative that I should stay in London. It was then my intention to proceed immediately to Monte Carlo, to commence operations; and, my fortune restored to me, to join my dear wife, and commence a new life.

"Of all this she, of course, knew nothing. Ignorant of the real cause of my downfall, how could she have divined the truth? Had there been that confidence between us which should exist between man and wife, I might at this moment be different from what I am. I should not be, as I am, bowed down with a sense of guilt from which my soul can never be cleansed. It was not she who was at fault, but I. Had I confided to her, had she been really aware where and in what company I spent my nights, she would have been spared the agony of a belief which, out of charity to me, she would not shame me and herself by revealing. So we two stood on the platform bidding a cold farewell to each other, each tortured by a secret we dared not confess. I kissed her, and kissed my sweet Clair.

"'Do come with us, papa!' said Clair, nestling in my arms.

"My wife looked up into my face appealingly. In that one moment, had I seized the opportunity, there was still a chance of redemption.

"'Robert!' she said, involuntarily raising her hands and clasping them.

"Ah, if I had met her appeal! If I had said: 'Do not go by this train; I will confess everything to you!' But the prompting did not come to me; if it had, I should have disregarded it.

"'I cannot come with you, Clair,' I said; 'I have such a deal to do before I leave London.'

"'Poor papa!' she said. 'That is why you keep out so late at night. Poor papa!'

"My wife turned her head from us, but I saw the scarlet blush on her face, which I attributed to her displeasure at my refusal. Or was it that she suspected my secret?

"'You have not betrayed me?' I said apart to my friend. 'She does not know how I have lost my fortune, and what has brought me to this?'

"'On my honor, no,' he answered. 'She has not the least suspicion of your stupid infatuation.'

"'You will not call it stupid in three or four weeks,' I said.

"'It is not possible for your system to fail?' he questioned.

"'There isn't the remotest possibility of it,' I replied. 'Clever people think that everything has been found out about figures and chances. I am going to show them something new.'

"The whistle sounded; the guard bade the passengers take their places. I walked along the platform as the train moved away. Clair waved her handkerchief to me; my friend nodded good-by; my wife did not raise her head to look at me.

"I hastened back to my house, and found the broker there. He was a wealthy dealer, and was going through the rooms when I entered, appraising everything and putting down figures. I accompanied him from one room to another, and we smoked as he made his calculations. I was impatient and unhappy, but he would not be hurried. He opened the door of my wife's morning-room; I pulled him back.

"'Not this room?' he asked.

"'Pshaw!' I said. 'Everything must go.'

"There were some small things in the room which seemed to me to have so close a personal relation to my wife that I was angry to see him handle them. Why had she not taken these things away with her? She might have spared me the reproach. I walked out of the room while he valued them.

"At length his catalogue was ended.

"'You want the money immediately?' he asked.

"'Immediately,' I replied.

"'A check will do, of course.'

"'No, I must have cash.'

"'That will make a slight difference,' he said, and he named the amount he was willing to give me. It was less than I anticipated, but the business worried me, and I agreed. Saying he would return in an hour and complete the bargain, he left me.

"I was alone in the house to which I had brought my wife, a bride. All the servants had been paid off, and had left. I had arranged this because I could not endure that they should see the sacrifice I was making. Memories of the past rushed upon me—of my young wife's delight as I took her through the rooms, of the fond endearments at my cleverness and forethought, of the happy evening we passed, sitting in the gloaming and talking of the future. Alas, the future! How fearful the contrast between my young bride's fond imaginings and the reality! In solitary communing I strolled through the rooms and marked each spot and each article hallowed by some cherished recollection. The piano at which she used to sit and sing in the early days of our marriage, the window from which we used to watch the sunset, the small articles on her dressing-table—there seemed to be a living spirit in them that greeted me reproachfully, and asked, 'Why have you done this? Why have you blighted that fair young life?' Our Clair was born in the house. The cot in which she slept was there, her favorite child-pictures hung upon the wall. What pangs went through me as I surveyed the wreck of bright hopes! 'But I will atone for it,' I said inwardly. 'When fortune is mine once more I will confess all, and ask my dear wife's forgiveness. Then, then for the happy future!' No warning whispers reached me. No voice cried,' Sinner and fool! You have done what can never be undone. Not only fortune, but love, is lost forever!'

"If I dwell upon these small matters, Rathbeal, it is because the impressions of that lonely hour are as strong within me now as then, and because they are pregnant with an awful lesson.

"The hour over, the broker returned with wagons and men. As he paid me the money his workmen commenced to remove the furniture. I left the house to their mercies, and went to meet the men to whom I was indebted. I paid them to the last shilling, and, honor satisfied, was master of a sum sufficiently large, I thought, to carry on my operations at Monte Carlo. I played at the club that night, and lost a few pounds. It did not affect me; I was rather glad, indeed, for it pointed to the road where wealth awaited me. I had taken a bed in a hotel, but an impulse seized me to visit my house once more. It was two in the morning when I turned the key and lit the hall gas. My footsteps resounded on the dusky passages. The broker had been expeditious; everything in the house was removed, and I seemed to be walking through a hollow grave—but it was a grave, haunted by ghostly shadows, eloquent with accusing voices. I shut my eyes, I put my hands to my ears, but I still saw the ghostly shadows and heard the accusing voices. I rushed from the house, conscience-stricken and appalled.

"The next morning my courage returned; the sun shone brightly, and I had money, and my system, in my pocket. Away, then, to Monte Carlo, to redeem the past!

"I did not commence immediately; I studied the tables, the croupiers, the players, and I spent several hours in going over the figures and combinations I had prepared. Then I took the plunge.

"As is frequently the case, I was successful at first; in four days I doubled my capital. My friend came to see me, as I had requested him to do, to give me news of my wife. She had not written to me, and I asked him the reason; he said he was not acquainted with the reason, and he asked me how I was progressing. I showed him, exultingly, what I had done; he expressed surprise and satisfaction.

"'How long will it take you to accomplish your aim?' he asked.

"'If I play as I am playing now,' I replied, 'some two or three weeks. If I play more boldly, a week may accomplish it.'

"'Why not play boldly?' he suggested.

"I had half intended to do so, and his words encouraged me. We went to the tables together, and I began to plunge. Before I left the rooms I had lost all I had won, and some part of the money I had brought with me. I pretended to make light of it.

"'These adverse combinations occasionally occur," I said, 'but they right themselves infallibly if you hold on. It is only a temporary repulse.'

"But though I spoke confidently my heart was fainting within me. Theory is one thing, practice another. We can be very bold on paper, but when we are fighting with the enemy we feel his blows.

"The next day my friend accompanied me again to the tables, With all my boasting I had not the daring to risk my capital in half-a-dozen bold coups; I put on much smaller sums, and I had the mortification of learning that my want of courage prevented me from winning what I ought to have done.

"'You see,' I said to my friend. 'Faint heart never succeeded yet. But it is only a little time lost, and it proves the certainty of my calculations.'

"He had to leave me that evening, and he made me promise that I would write to him daily of my progress. As he was going to see my wife, I gave him a letter to her, in which I begged her to write to me at Monte Carlo. He said he would deliver the letter, and it was not until some time afterward that I recalled his manner as being somewhat strained.

"The story of the next few days is soon told. Hope, despair; hope again, followed by despair. I came down to my last hundred pounds. Over and over again, in the solitude of my room, I proved to myself how weak I had been in not doing this or that at the right moment; over and over again I proved to my own misery that it was due to my own lack of courage that I had not won back my fortune. I conned the numbers I had written down as they were called out. 'Fool, fool, fool!' I cried, striking my forehead. 'Wretched, contemptible coward!' I rose in the morning haggard and weary; I had not slept a moment all the night. There was still a chance left: I had a hundred pounds; I would play on a lower martingale, and as I won I would increase it. I did so. That day I remained at the tables ten hours without rising from the seat I had secured. I won, I lost, I won again, I lost again. A few minutes before the rooms closed I had followed my system to a point whereat, after a series of losses, it needed but a large amount to be staked to get all back again. I had this amount before me. On previous occasions I had drawn back at such a critical juncture, and had suffered for it by hearing the number called which, in its various winning chances, would have recouped, with large profit, all that had been lost in the series. I would not be guilty of this cowardice again. With a trembling hand I put every franc I had on the various chances which were certain this time to win. The number was called. Great God! I was beggared! Without a word I rose and went to my hotel.

"Can you imagine the torments of hell, Rathbeal? I suffered them then. But there was worse in store for me.

76

"Figures, figures, figures, red and black, living figures that moved, that spoke, that glared and mocked me—the voices of the croupiers, the exclamations of the gamesters, the rattle of the money—curses and benedictions—now surrounded by a blaze of light, now plunged into black darkness—painted women, men with hideous faces, lips that smiled and derided—these were the images that haunted me in the night. I had drunk brandy, contrary to my usual habit, for I was never fond of drink, and my brain was burning. From time to time I dozed, and scarcely knew whether I was awake or asleep, whether what I saw were phantoms or actual forms of things. Was that a knock at my door? Was that the voice of a waiter speaking to me outside? I did not answer; I did not move. What mattered anything now? If the door opened, it could signify nothing to me; if some person entered and went away, there was no interest in the movements to beguile me from the tortures I was suffering. Ruin and I were company enough.

"The sun was streaming into my room long before I rose; when I got out of bed I staggered like a drunken man, though, except for the delirium of my senses, I was perfectly sober. It was not till I had washed and dressed that I observed a letter upon my table. Taking it up, I saw that it was in the handwriting of my wife.

"I hardly dared to open it; by my own act I had destroyed any claim to her affection. I had brought deep unhappiness upon her; I had systematically neglected her; I had lost the home which should have been hers; I had taken our child's money, and could not return it. But the letter must be read. With trembling hands I unfastened the envelope, and drew forth the sheet.

"It bore neither date nor address. I have the letter by me now, and I copy it word for word:

"I can bear my agony in silence no longer. I write to you, I speak to you, for the last time. This is my last farewell to him I loved, to the father of my child, to the husband who should have been my shield.

"Do you remember the words you addressed to me when we were married? 'I love you,' you said, 'I am your husband and lover. Nothing shall ever harm or wound you. I am your shield—the shield of love.'

"With what fondness I used to repeat these words to myself! My shield! My shield of love! Side by side with my worship of the Eternal did I worship you, as the realization of a young girl's happiest dreams; my joy, my hope, my shield of love!

"Slowly, slowly did I awake from my dream. I would not, I could not, believe what you were showing me day by day, but the terrible truth forced itself upon me with power so resistless, with conviction so absolute, that I could no longer refuse to believe. How bitter was the knowledge, how bitter, how bitter!

"I gave you all my love. But for your own actions it would never have wavered. O Richard! if in a moment of temptation you had turned to me, I might have been your shield, as you promised to be mine!

"I know your secret. I have known it for years—for long, bitter years. I cannot blame myself that I did not satisfy your expectations. All that a loving woman could do I did to retain your love. I hid nothing from you; I strove with all my might to make your home pleasant and attractive to you; what power lay within me to keep you faithful to the vows we pledged was exercised by me to the utmost of my abilities. I used to say to myself, 'What can I do to win my husband's society and confidence? How can I act so that he shall not continue to grow weary of me?' You will never know how hard I strove, you will never know the tears I shed as I slowly recognized that my shield of love was a mockery, and that there was as little loving meaning in your declaration as if it had been uttered by a deadly enemy.

"Yes, Richard, I know your secret; I know that you have not been faithful to me; I know that for years your heart has been given to another. I cannot say that I hope you will be happy with her who occupies my place. At this solemn moment I will not be guilty of a subterfuge. The issue lies in God's hand, not in mine, nor in yours.

"I should not address this farewell to you if it were not that I feel I have not long to live. It is grief that is killing me, not a mortal disease which doctors can minister to.

"It is with distinct purpose that I put no address to this farewell. I have left the place I went to when you bade me good-by in London, and it is my desire that you shall not know where I am, that you shall not come to me. Remorse may touch your soul, and you may wish to come; but it would not be a sincere wish, springing, as it must, from a sudden false feeling of compassion in which there is no truth or depth. How could I believe what you said, after all the years of suffering I have gone through? And as a wife I must preserve my self-respect. Coming to me from a woman for whom you deserted me, I would not receive you. It is long since I bade farewell to happiness. I now bid farewell to you."

"That was all. Many times did I pause to question myself, and to read again, in doubt whether I had mistaken the words. That the accusation my wife brought against me was untrue you may believe, Rathbeal. No woman had won me from her side, and I was so far innocent. That, ignorant of the true cause of my neglect, she may have had grounds for suspicion, I could well believe, but she seemed to speak with something more than suspicion. Who had maligned me? Who had played me false? And for what purpose?

"I could think of no one. At times during my degraded career in London I had had disagreements with the men I played with, but I could not convict one of them with any degree of certainty.

"The postmark on the envelope was Paris, and there was but one means of ascertaining my wife's address—through the only friend I had in the world. To go to her, beggared as I was, would be adding shame to shame. Besides, I could not pay my hotel bill. But still it impressed itself upon me as an imperative duty that I should find her and make full confession; and then to bid her farewell forever.

"I wrote to my friend, to his address in London; I made a strong appeal to him, and informed him of the position I was in. He wrote back after a delay of two days; he said he had something of a very grave nature to attend to that would take him from England, and he could not, therefore, come to me at once. When he saw me he would inform me why he could not come earlier. I was to remain where I was till he arrived; he would be responsible for my hotel bill; I was not to trouble myself about that. I learned from the landlord that he had received a letter from my friend, making himself responsible for my debt to him.

"'You have had a turn of ill luck at the tables,' said the landlord. 'It is the way with most gentlemen; but sometimes a turn comes the other way.' He appeared perfectly satisfied, but I could not help feeling that he regarded me as a personal hostage for the amount of the bill.

"I wrote again to my friend, imploring him not to delay, and this time I received no answer to my letter. I supposed he had left England on the business he referred to, and in my helpless position I was compelled to wait and eat my heart away.

"Ten days elapsed before he came; he was dressed in mourning, and was sad and anxious, as though he had passed through some deep trouble.

"'It was impossible for me to get here before,' he said gravely.

"I nodded impatiently, and then, with an awkward, consciousness that something was due to him, I touched his black coat.

"'You have had a loss,' I said.

"'You will hear sad news presently,' he answered, 'and you must prepare yourself for it. But tell me first of your troubles here. I was so harassed and grieved at the time your letter arrived that I hardly understood it; and then I laid it aside and could not find it again.'

"Curbing my impatience, for he insisted upon my exposing the full extent of my misfortunes, I related to him briefly the result of my mad venture.

"'And you are utterly ruined?' he said.

"'Utterly, utterly ruined,' I replied. 'Enough of myself for the present. Tell me of my wife.'

"His countenance fell. There was a significance in his manner which profoundly agitated me. Eager for an answer, and dreading it, I asked him why he did not speak.

"'It is cruel,' he murmured, his face still averted from me, 'at such a time, when you have lost every hope in life, to say what I have come to say. We will speak together to-morrow.'

"'We will speak together now!' I cried, seizing him by the arm, and compelling him to turn toward me. 'Do you think that anything you can say, any message you may bring from her, can add to the misery and degradation of my position? Tell me of my wife!'

"'How can I speak?' he murmured. 'What can I say?'

"'Speak the truth,' I said, 'and do not spare me. I deserve no mercy. I had none upon her; I cannot expect her to have any upon me. But an imputation has been cast upon me, an infamous, revolting imputation, and I must clear myself of it. That done, I shall not care what becomes of me. I have not told you of the last letter I received from her, the only letter she has written to me since we parted. In that letter she brings a horrible charge against me, instigated by some villain who bears me ill will, and I insist upon my right to defend myself.'

"I would have said more, but my emotion overpowered me.

"'She will not hear you,' said my friend sadly.

"'She has told me so in her letter,' I replied; 'but you can give me her address, and I will write to her.'

"'It will be useless,' he said, 'quite useless, I grieve to say.'

"'You mean that she will return the letter to me unopened; but I will not rest until she receives my denial of the crime of which she believes me guilty.'

"'She will never receive it,' he said in a solemn tone. 'Cannot you guess the truth?'

"'Good God!' I cried, a despairing light breaking upon me.

"'I can keep it from you no longer,' said my friend; 'sooner or later it must be spoken. She had been for a long time in bad health, as you know; it was impossible to disguise it—her state was serious. The only hope for her lay in a change of climate and in perfect freedom from mental anxiety. In my answer to your letter informing me of your misfortunes at this fatal place I told you I had something of a grave nature to attend to. It concerned your wife. A secret sorrow which she did not impart to me had aggravated her condition, which had become so alarming that the doctor held out no hope of recovery. She had another terrible grief to contend with. Your child—but I cannot go on.'

"'You must go on. My wife—my Clair!—'

"He assisted me to a seat; I was too weak to stand.

"'Go on,' I muttered. 'Go on. All must be told—all, all! Do not spare me. Let me know the worst.'

"'Grave symptoms had developed themselves in Clair,' he continued, 'and it was feared that she would share the fate that awaited your wife. In these distressing circumstances she called upon me, and I went to her without delay. I was shocked at her appearance. Death was in her face; death was in the face of your child! I begged her to let me send for you. She would not hear of it; it terrified me to hear the vehemence of her refusal. "He shall not look upon me again, dead or alive!" she cried. "He shall not look upon my child! We are parted for ever and ever!" The doctor, coming in at that moment, warned me that opposition to anything upon which she had set her heart would snap the frail cord that bound her to life. "She can survive but a short time," he said. "In mercy to her, let her last moments be peaceful." What could I say—what could I do but obey?'

"My friend waited for my answer. 'You did what was right,' I murmured, racked with anguish. 'Was she at this time in the village she went to when we parted?'

"'She had removed from it without my knowledge, in order that you should not find her. It grieves me to make these revelations to you, but the time has gone by for concealment. Clair died first. Her death was painless.'

"'Did she not speak? Did she not ask for me?'

"'She spoke no word that I could hear. She passed away with her lips to her mother's face. "I am glad my Clair has gone first," your wife said. "It would have pained me to leave her alone in this cruel world. She is safe now; she has not lived to have her heart broken. She is waiting for me, and I shall join her soon—very soon!" I remained with her to the last. Believe me when I say I would have written to you had she not bound me by a solemn obligation which I dared not break. She demanded an oath from me, and to ease her aching heart I gave it. I could not, I could not refuse her. She died on the following day. Your wife and child lie in one grave.'

"'Where?' I found voice to ask.

"'I dare not tell you. Not for any worldly consideration will I be false to the dead. Again she made me swear that absolute secrecy should be preserved as to her last resting-place. "I should not rest in my grave," she said, "if my husband stood above it." I implore you not to press me, for I will not, I cannot be false to my trust. Alas, that I should be compelled to say this to the friend of my youth! You know the worst now. There is nothing more to tell.'

"It was just; it was what I had earned. Of what avail would tears have been, shed over the cold earth that covered the forms of my wife and child? I had tortured them for years, and I was justly punished.

"'She sent me no message?' I asked, after a long pause.

"'None; and she made no distinct complaint against you. All that she said was that her heart was broken, and that she left the world gladly. It is the saddest of news, but we reap as we sow.'

"I acknowledged it. As I had sown, so had I reaped. What better harvest could I have expected? Desolate and alone I stood upon the shore, without kith or kin. It was with a stern satisfaction that I thought I should not remain long on earth. It was truly my impression at that time; I had the firmest belief that my hours were numbered.

"'You will make no attempt,' said my friend, 'to discover where they are laid?'

"'Her wishes shall be respected,' I said gloomily. 'I could have brought no comfort to her or to my child had they lived. I will not disturb them now they are gone.'

"'It is due from you, I think,' he said, and presently added, 'What will you do now?'

"'With my life?' I asked; and then I told him what I believed, that I had not long to live. 'But for the short time that yet remains to me I cut myself entirely away from all personal associations with men and women whom I have known. I renounce even the name I bear, to avoid recognition, and shall assume another. I am as one who has died, and who commences life anew. If by my actions during the days that yet may be mine I can atone in some small measure for the guilt that lies upon my soul, such atonements shall be made. It is likely I may not reside in England; the recollections that would force themselves upon me there would be too painful to bear.'

"He approved of my resolution, and offered to render me some small regular assistance to assist me to live. I accepted it after some hesitation; he had made money out of me while acting as my steward, and I thought he could afford it. Should I find myself master of more than would be requisite for the barest necessaries, I would devote it to the children of misery in memory of my wife, who had a charitable heart, and was always giving to the poor. But what sweet virtue could be named that did not grace her soul?

"You know now, Rathbeal, how it was that I did not bear my own name when you first became acquainted with me. It was by chance that you made this discovery, and it was partly because I felt that there was a cowardice in the subterfuge, and that I was practicing it to avoid the moral punishment I had earned, that when we were together abroad I resumed my own. There was no need to make my friend acquainted with this, and it is probable that he is in ignorance of it to this day. It does not in any way concern him. I have cut myself away from him as I have done from every person who knew me during my wife's lifetime. The motive that induced me to request you to inform him that he would be troubled with me no more was this: I had to some extent bound myself to him not to return to England, and when I resolved to do so in your company I felt that I was partially violating that understanding. Consequently I determined to sever all personal relations between him and myself. He has not sought me, nor shall I ever seek him. Our ways of life lie widely apart, and it is hardly likely we shall ever meet again. He believes me probably to be dead; let him rest in this belief.

"I have nothing to add, Rathbeal, to this lengthy confession. You know the worst of me. If you condemn me be silent, it will be charitable. If I am still allowed to retain your friendship, it will ease my heart.

"Robert Grantham."

CHAPTER IX.

Mr. Fox-Cordery is not easy in his mind.

In a state of deep dissatisfaction with the world in general, Mr. Fox-Cordery paced the lawn fronting the country house he had taken on the banks of the Thames. He was smoking one of his fragrant cigars, but it had no soothing effect upon him; a common weed of British make would have afforded him as much gratification. He was perplexed and annoyed, and was growing savage; and yet he had cause, if not for gratitude—of which it may be doubted whether he was capable—at least for self-congratulation.

To commence with the credit side of his ledger, here he was comfortably installed in the house facing the river of which we have heard his mother speak, with its piece of meadow-land, and its lawn, and its garden of fruit and flowers, and its rustic bridge stretching to a bank on the opposite side. This bridge, being erected over an inlet, did not interfere with the traffic of the river proper, and was a decided attraction to the summer residence which Mr. Fox-Cordery had taken to carry out a long cherished design. The arm of water it spanned was deep, and upon it was floating a gayly-painted boat, bearing in gilt letters the name, "Lucy and Clair." He had so christened it in honor of the guests he was entertaining, Mrs. Grantham and her little daughter. He had intended to call it simply "Lucy"; but love is sometimes wanting in boldness, and for this reason, or because he was not sure of his ground, he had associated the names of mother and daughter, which he considered the lady he was scheming to win could not but regard as a delicate mark of attention.

To go on with, his mind was more at ease with respect to the fate of the friend he had betrayed than it had been on the day of his interviews with John Dixon and Rathbeal. Six weeks had passed by and he had not seen or heard from John Dixon: a distinct proof that that astute person had been gasconading when he spoke of having caught a glimpse of Robert Grantham's face on a foggy night in March. Mr. Fox-Cordery had arrived at the conclusion that the tale was a clumsy invention, introduced for the purpose of winning compliance with John Dixon's suit for the hand of his sister Charlotte.

"Dixon thought I would strike my flag," he reasoned, "and that I would implore him to take Charlotte at once, and a handsome dowry with her, as the price of his silence. A likely thing when he had nothing to sell but an empty tale!" Of the legacy he had heard nothing more. Mrs. Grantham had not seen the advertisement in the _Times_, the paper being one which she did not read, nor had she been approached by the lawyers with respect to it, as had been threatened by John Dixon. "Lawyers don't part with money too readily," again reasoned Mr. Fox-Cordery, "when once it gets into their clutches. I know their tricks."

Then, Charlotte was behaving admirably. She and Mrs. Grantham and Clair were constantly together, Mr. Fox-Cordery believed that his sister was doing something—perhaps in an indirect way, but that was of no account—to advance his cause. And yet that cause was making no progress. It was unaccountable, and he was moodily reflecting upon this as he paced the lawn and smoked his cigar.

On the debit side of the ledger were some ridiculous, though mysterious, eccentricities on the part of Rathbeal. Rathbeal did not appear personally, but he kept himself in Mr. Fox-Cordery's mind by a series of written and pictorial communications. These, carefully sealed, were addressed to Mr. Fox-Cordery's London residence, and were forwarded on to his suburban home. He destroyed them, wrathfully, almost as soon as he received them, but it was an additional annoyance that he could not forget them after they were destroyed; indeed, the impression they produced was so strong that they were the cause of many fantastic and disturbing dreams from which he would awake in perturbation. The peculiar nature of these communications will be seen from the following examples:

"When you weave a web, shrewd sir," wrote Rathbeal, quoting an observation made by Mr. Fox-Cordery in the course of their recent interview, "nothing ever escapes from it."

(Signed) "Rathbeal."

Beneath these words was the picture of a large web, in a corner of which lurked a spider, bearing an unmistakable likeness to Mr. Fox-Cordery. A number of unfortunate creatures, with human faces, struggled in the meshes. The face of one figure, designated Fate, was hidden, purposely it seemed.

Again, after an interval of a few days:

"There are other webs than those that mortals weave," wrote Rathbeal, quoting his reply to Mr. Fox-Cordery's observation. "Fate is ever at work.

(Signed) "Rathbeal."

Beneath this was the same web, but this time Mr. Fox-Cordery was in the meshes, struggling in terror to release himself; while in the corner lurked the figure of Fate, still with its face hidden.

"The man is crazy," was Mr. Fox-Cordery's comment, "or in his dotage."

Nevertheless he could not banish these sketches from his mind, and he found himself wondering who the figure with his hidden face was intended to represent.

At intervals came couplets of verse:

The bark we steer has stranded. O breeze, auspicious swell:
We yet may see once more the friend we love so well.

"For auspicious," wrote Rathbeal, "read malefic. For love, read hate."

At another time:

Better the drunkard void of fraud and wiles
Than virtue's braggart who by fraud beguiles.

Another post brought:

What serves thy armor 'gainst Fate's arrows fierce?
What serves thy shield if Destiny transpierce?

Had Mr. Fox-Cordery not been sensible of the advisability of silence he might have taken fighting notice of these missives, which, in their frequency, savored of persecution. He was tempted, as his eyes fell upon the familiar writing on the envelope, to tear and burn it, unopened, but he had not the nerve to do this; he was possessed with a strange fear that it might contain some news of importance to himself, and thus he was made to contribute to his own uneasiness.

But these were small matters in comparison with the one desire of which he had become the slave. In the retreat he had chosen he had hoped to attain his wish, and to win from Mrs. Grantham a promise that she would become his wife. Long as he had loved her, he had not had the courage to speak to her openly. Many times had he approached the boundary line which stood between friendship and love, and had never dared to cross it. Something in her manner, which he could not define or satisfactorily explain to himself, deterred him; and he lacked the gamester's mettle to risk his all upon the hazard of the die. He argued with himself that she could scarcely mistake the meaning of the attentions he was paying her during this visit. Daily offerings of flowers, a constant ministering to her pleasure, fulfillment of any wish she expressed, the most careful attention to the adornment of his small person, a display of amiability to her, to Charlotte and his mother, and even to the servants who waited on them—all these efforts seemed to be thrown away upon her. As has been stated, he was growing savage to find his meaning thus misunderstood, his desire thus frustrated. Had he seen her while he was restlessly and moodily pacing the lawn and been able to read what was passing within her, he might have arrived at a better understanding of the position of affairs; and had he witnessed a scene which was presently to take place between Mrs. Grantham and his sister Charlotte, it would not have assisted in comforting him.

Mrs. Grantham was alone in her room. It was Charlotte's birthday, and she was looking in her trunk for a gift she designed to give her friend, a brooch of turquoise and pearls which she herself had worn as a young girl. The brooch was in a desk which lay at the bottom of the trunk, and it was seldom she opened it, for it contained mementos of the past which it pained her to handle; but they were dear to her despite the pain they caused her, and she would not have parted with them for untold gold. Lifting the desk from the trunk, she rose with it in her hands and seated herself at a table.

The deep sorrow of her life had left its traces on her face, had touched her eyes with an abiding sadness; but a delicate beauty dwelt there still. Charlotte, who had insisted upon being her handmaiden, and had begged to be allowed to attend her when she retired to bed, would comment admiringly upon the graces of her person, comments which Mrs. Grantham would receive with gentle deprecation. Until late years Charlotte had known nothing of Mrs. Grantham, and was even now as ignorant of her history as she was of the close association which had existed between her and her brother. During the present visit a fond confidence was established between the women, and each knew that in the other she possessed a true and faithful friend. But Mrs. Grantham had not admitted Charlotte into the secrets of her married life. The anguish and indignation which had tortured her soul when she learned from Mr. Fox-Cordery that her husband was unfaithful to her had long since passed away. Death had consecrated her grief, and had robbed it of its bitter sting.

Mrs. Grantham unlocked her desk. In a small box, at the top of two or three packets of letters, were the brooch and a few ornaments she used to wear in happier days. She placed the brooch aside, and taking out the other articles of jewelry, gazed at them with yearning tenderness. They were chiefly gifts which her husband had given her during their courtship and the first few months of their marriage. Since she had received the news of her husband's death from the lips of Mr. Fox-Cordery she had not worn an ornament he had given her; and the only ring upon her fingers was her wedding ring, which had never been removed. But she had preserved them all, even the smallest article, and every letter he had written to her was in the desk, carefully folded and preserved. An impulse stirred her to untie the packets and read the endearing words he had addressed to her, and for a moment she was inclined to yield to it, but she went no farther than to place her fingers on the ribbon which held them together. With a sigh she replaced the packets in the desk, but not before she had put her lips to them. Her husband, living, had sorely wronged her, but when she heard that he was dead she forgave him, and did not thereafter allow her thoughts to dwell upon any remembrances of him that were not tender and kind. He had sinned, and had suffered for his sin. She could not carry resentment beyond the grave. And he was the father of her child, the sweetest hope the world contained for her.

When her trunk was repacked the turquoise and pearl brooch was not the only ornament she had retained, There was a ring of gold set with one black pearl which her husband used to wear. One day she had expressed admiration of it, and he had had it made smaller for her. She put it on her finger now, and pressed her lips to it. As she did so her eyes filled with tears.

"May I come in?"

It was Charlotte's voice, following a tap at the door.

"Yes, come in, dear."

Charlotte entered, a different young woman from the last occasion upon which we saw her. She was neatly dressed, and her eyes were sparkling and her face radiant.

"A happy birthday to you, dear," said Mrs. Grantham. "Let me fasten this on."

Charlotte had never possessed a gold ornament of any kind, and her eyes fairly danced as she looked at herself in the glass.

"For me, Mrs. Grantham? Really for me?"

"Yes, dear. It was one I used to wear when I was a girl, and I thought you would like it."

"Like it! I shall love it all my life. Do you know, Mrs. Grantham, it is the first brooch I have ever had!"

"You don't mean that? And you twenty-nine to-day!"

"Yes, I am not a girl, as you were when you wore it. I am not at all sorry to be twenty-nine, for I think no one is happier than I am."

The fact is Charlotte had received this morning the tenderest letter from John Dixon, wishing her happiness and every good on earth, He had bought a birthday gift for her (said John Dixon), but it had required a little alteration, and to his annoyance the man who was making the alteration had disappointed him; but he was after him like a tiger (said John Dixon), and she should have the token that very morning, or he would know the reason why. John Dixon always wrote to Charlotte in good spirits, and in this birthday letter he was at his blithest.

"It takes very little to make you happy," observed Mrs. Grantham, looking rather thoughtfully at Charlotte, who was exhibiting, not the pleasure of a woman at her gift, but the delight of a child.

"Do you call this very little?" asked Charlotte, gayly. "I call it a great deal."

"Charlotte," said Mrs. Grantham, "did not your mother or your brother ever give you a brooch, or a bracelet, or any little thing of the kind?"

Charlotte was on her guard instantly. She had felt during the past few weeks that much depended upon her mother and brother, and that they expected her to speak of them at their best. Therefore she was uncertain what to say in answer to Mrs. Grantham's straight question.

"But tell me, dear," urged Mrs. Grantham, "did you never have such a gift?"

"Do not ask me," replied Charlotte. "I must not say anything unkind."

"It is an answer, dear," said Mrs. Grantham, with a pitying smile. "I have noticed that you never wear the smallest ornament."

"Nor do you; only your wedding ring. And now I declare you have another ring on! Is it a pearl?"

"Yes, Charlotte. It is a ring my husband gave me. I have not worn any jewels since his death, but I have a number in my desk."

"And you have put it on to-day in remembrance."

"Yes, dear, in remembrance."

She was on the point of saying that she did not wish to continue the subject, but she was reminded that this would afford Charlotte a valid excuse for not giving her some information which she was now desirous to obtain.

She had not been quite oblivious of the attentions which Mr. Fox-Cordery was paying her, and although she had marked out her course of life, she had lately become not only curious concerning him, but doubtful. Upon her first introduction to Charlotte she had observed the menial dress the young woman wore, and the want of affection displayed toward her in her home. Mr. Fox-Cordery and his mother had not been careful to disguise their feelings in her presence, and it was pity and sympathy for Charlotte which had attracted her. She afterward learned to love Charlotte for her own sake, and it was chiefly because of Charlotte's pleadings that she had been induced to accept the invitation which led to her present visit. And in this closer association she had grown to love the young woman more.

Never before had Charlotte the opportunity of unbosoming herself to one of her own sex, to one in whom she felt she could confide. In their walks together, she and her little Clair and Charlotte, constant evidences of Charlotte's kindness of heart and humane instincts had presented themselves to her, and she more than once suspected that here was a well which never yet had had free play. The information that this little brooch was the first gift of any value that Charlotte could call her own caused her to reflect. That a being so tender and kind should be treated with so much neglect gave her a shock.

"Dear Mrs. Grantham," said Charlotte, "how you must have suffered when you lost your dear husband! I can imagine it. I should wish to die."

"There was my little Clair left to me, dear; and life means, not love alone, but duty. I am glad I lived to take care of my child. Do you expect to be married soon, Charlotte?"

"Some time this year, I think."

"When in your position, dear, one thinks one generally knows. I should not be a false prophet if I said for certain this year."

"I think it will be."

"I have not seen your intended, dear."

"He is noble and good," said Charlotte, enthusiastically.

"And loves you with his whole heart, as you love him."

"Yes, it is truly so."

The women kissed each other.

"You must introduce me to him," said Mrs. Grantham, "when he comes to London."

"Oh, but he is in London," said Charlotte simply. "He lives here."

Mrs. Grantham looked at her in astonishment.

"But why does he not visit you?"

Charlotte's face grew scarlet; she dared not answer the question.

"Never mind, dear," said Mrs. Grantham, pitying her confusion; "but you understand that I wish to know him, for your sake."

"I understand. Mrs. Grantham, I ought not to keep anything from you. The reason why Mr. Dixon does not come to see me here, is that he and my brother are not exactly friends. They had a disagreement in business, and that is how the trouble occurred. Do not say anything to my brother about it; it might make him angry."

"With me, dear?"

"Oh, no," said Charlotte, without thinking, "he could not be angry with you."

"With you, then?" said Mrs. Grantham, her mind half on Charlotte and half on herself.

"I don't know how it is," said Charlotte, in a tone of distress, "but I seem to be saying things I ought not to speak of. If I were clever it would not happen."

"You are clever, dear, and you are good; that is why I love you."

"If I only thought that what I have said without intending it, and what perhaps I have made you think without intending it, wouldn't make you run away from us—"

"I will not run away, Charlotte. If you wish it, I will stay as long as I have promised."

"I do wish it; with all my heart I wish it. I never had a friend like you; I never had a sister—"

But here Charlotte quite broke down; her sobs would not allow her to proceed.

"There, there, dear," said Mrs. Grantham, soothing her. "Tears on your birthday! Why, Charlotte, what are you thinking of? And with a true friend by your side—!"

"I know, I know," murmured Charlotte. "I am very ungrateful."

"You are a dear, loveable young woman, and you have won my heart. And who knows whether I may not be able to help you just where you most need help? There is a knock at the door. Don't move; no one must catch you crying, or they will have a bad opinion of me. I will go and see who it is."

It was a maid with a little parcel for Charlotte.

"I was to give it to Miss Fox-Cordery at once, ma'am," said the maid, "and I was told she was in your room."

"She is here," said Mrs. Grantham, "and she shall have it immediately."

The maid departed, and Mrs. Grantham locked the door, so as to be secure from intrusion.

"Something for you, dear. I guess a birthday present."

"Oh!" cried Charlotte eagerly, starting to her feet and holding out her hand.

"The question is, from whom," said Mrs. Grantham, with tender playfulness.

"I know!" said Charlotte, still more eagerly.

"From your brother?"

Charlotte shook her head rather sadly.

"From your mother?"

Another sad shake of Charlotte's head.

"They have given you something already, perhaps!"

"No, Mrs. Grantham; I do not expect anything from them. They do not make birthday presents."

"Don't think I want to tease you; I only want to find out how I can best serve you. I will not keep you in suspense any longer. Here it is, dear."

Charlotte opened the packet clumsily, her fingers trembled so, and disclosed a tiny note and a small jewel case. The note ran:

My Dear Charlotte: Accept this, with my fond and constant love. Ever yours, JOHN.

The jewel case contained a ring of diamonds. The tears that glistened now in Charlotte's eyes were tears of joy.

"An engagement ring, I should say," said Mrs. Grantham, gayly. "I want more than ever to be friends with John. And it fits perfectly. Now, how did John manage that?" Her mood changed from gayety to tender solicitude. She drew Charlotte to her side. "I wish you a happy life, dear. Take a piece of advice from a friend who has had experiences: When you are married have no secrets from your husband. Trust him unreservedly; conceal nothing from him. If you note any change in him that causes you uneasiness do not brood over it in silence; ask him frankly the reason, and if he is reluctant to give it, implore him to confide in you. In married life there is no true happiness unless full confidence exists between husband and wife. And if the man is true and the woman is true, they should be to each other a shield of love, a protection against evil, a solace in the hour of sorrow."

"I will remember what you say, Mrs. Grantham. I hope Fox will not be displeased. He is not friends with John, and I have never worn a ring; and this is so grand and beautiful—"

"Never meet trouble, dear. Perhaps I shall have an opportunity of saying something to your brother to-day."

Charlotte looked at her and hesitated; there was something on her tongue to which she did not venture to give utterance. Knowing it was her brother's wish to make Mrs. Grantham his wife, she wondered whether any words to that end had passed between them. To call Mrs. Grantham sister would be a great happiness to her, but she trembled to think of the price at which that happiness would be bought. The oppression to which she herself had been subjected in her home since her father's death rose before her. Was such a fate in store for Mrs. Grantham? Was it not her duty to warn her? But she dared not speak; she could only hope that nothing had been settled, and that her dear friend would be spared unhappiness.

"Of what are you thinking, dear?" asked Mrs. Grantham, perceiving that a struggle was going on in Charlotte's heart.

"Of nothing," Charlotte replied, and inwardly prayed for courage to warn her before it was too late.

CHAPTER X.

In which Mr. Fox-Cordery meets with a repulse.

Shortly afterward Mr. Fox-Cordery saw Mrs. Grantham issue from the house and advance toward him. With conspicuous gallantry he went to meet her, and raised his hat. He was careful to omit no form of politeness and attention to establish himself in her regard.

"I have come especially to have a chat with you," said Mrs. Grantham, declining the arm he offered her. "Such old friends as ourselves need not stand upon ceremony."

Mr. Fox-Cordery looked upon this as a promising opening.

"There is something I wish to say to you," he said boldly and tenderly, "if you will listen to me."

"Certainly I will listen to you. Is it about business?"

"It is of far more importance than business," he replied, with a significance of tone that could not fail to convey some perception of his meaning.

She paused awhile before she spoke again, and then seemed to have arrived at a decision.

"I wish to say a word about your sister."

"Dear Charlotte!" he murmured, and could not have said anything, nor uttered what he said in a tone that would have been more fatal to his cause, even if she were willing to listen to it favorably. He had been his own enemy, and had forged the weapon that was to strike him down; for it was Mrs. Grantham's insight into the life Charlotte must have led with him and her mother that had made her reflect upon the true nature of the man who had been for so many years her husband's friend and her own. The closer intimacy of the last few weeks had served him ill. Mrs. Grantham was a lady of much sweetness, but the trials she had passed through had taught her to observe and sometimes to suspect.

"To-day is Charlotte's birthday," she said.

"Charlotte's birthday!" he exclaimed. "How could we have overlooked it? Charlotte's birthday! Why so it is! I must wish her every happiness." He began to pick some flowers. "For Charlotte," he said.

"She will appreciate them. I have grown very fond of your sister."

"You could not say anything to make me happier—except—"

She nipped his tenderly suggested exception in the bud by continuing:

"She has the most amiable nature in the world—"

"No, no," he protested; "not the _most_ amiable nature in the world."

"And is so sweet-tempered and self-sacrificing—"

"She shares the best qualities of our family," he managed to get in.

"That I am as anxious for her happiness as you yourself can be. She has had two birthday presents, which have given her great pleasure, one especially." ("Confound her!" was Mr. Fox-Cordery's thought, as he bent over a dwarf rose tree. "Who has been making her birthday presents?") "I have given her a poor little brooch"—("That is one of the presents," thought Mr. Fox-Cordery, "and Clair has given her the other. Of course, of course." He was content that the gifts should have come from Mrs. Grantham and her little girl)—"and Mr. Dixon," continued Mrs. Grantham, "sent her an engagement ring."

Mr. Fox-Cordery looked suddenly up.

"Mr. Dixon!" he cried. "An engagement ring!"

"Yes," said Mrs. Grantham, ignoring his surprise, "a very beautiful ring. It is set with diamonds, and Charlotte, you may depend, put it on her finger at once. She must never take it off, at least till she is married. We foolish women, you know, have superstitions."

"Charlotte has been telling you a great deal about Mr. Dixon," said Mr. Fox-Cordery, striving to speak amiably, and not succeeding.

"Not a great deal; very little, indeed. It is only because I would have an answer to my questions that I learned anything at all. I have a common failing of my sex: I am intensely curious. And I am really annoyed, taking the interest I do in your sister, that I have not yet been introduced to Mr. Dixon. How is it that I have not been introduced to Mr. Dixon? Put a little forget-me-not in your posy; it means remembrance."

He obeyed her, and then took the bull by the horns.

"Mrs. Grantham," he said, "inspired by a hope I have entertained for many years, you must not remain in ignorance of our family secrets. I do not blame Charlotte for speaking to you about Mr. Dixon—"

"No," she gently interposed, "you must not blame her. We chat together every night before we retire, and little things come out in our conversation. If you must blame anybody, blame me, for it is entirely my fault that I know anything of her engagement. I teased it out of her."

"I regarded it as a family secret," he said. "The fact is—it pains me to make the statement—that neither my mother nor I quite approve of Mr. Dixon. You do not know him, and I do not wish to say anything against him. We are more likely to form a correct estimate of his character than Charlotte. We have a wider experience of human nature."

"Granted. But Charlotte has set her heart upon him, and he appears to have a very sincere love for her. But I am wrong, perhaps, in presuming to interfere in a matter which you say is a family secret. I was not aware of it when I commenced to speak to you. Forgive me."

"Dear Mrs. Grantham," he said, "do not distress me by saying that you are wrong. You are right, entirely right, in everything you do. I only wished to explain to you why it is that Mr. Dixon does not visit us. We have Charlotte's interests at heart, and if she insists upon having her way we shall not thwart her. Our hope will be that her marriage will turn out better than we anticipate. It is true that we put her upon probation for a time. We desired her—you can ask her for confirmation of my statement—to wait for two months before she finally committed herself, and she consented to do so. And now, Mrs. Grantham—"

"Pardon me," interrupted Mrs. Grantham; "let me justify myself completely. In speaking to you about your sister, I was prompted by my affection for her; she is not a young girl, and can to some extent judge for herself. We will not discuss Mr. Dixon, who is represented to me in two opposite lights. Let us hope for the best, and that her union with that gentleman will be a happy one. My own married life taught me much that brought sadness to my heart; I will pray that no shadow shall rest upon hers. But my sorrows have been softened by time, and I have a heavenly consolation in the love of my child, to whom, since I lost my husband, I have consecrated my life."

"Let that life," he said grandiloquently, "be consecrated to make another happy, as well as your darling child."

"No," she said firmly; "I am fixed in my resolve to form no other ties. Mr. Fox-Cordery, it would be a mere pretense for me to say I do not understand you. I beg you to go no farther—to say nothing more. You were my husband's friend; you are mine. Let us remain friends."

"But, dear Mrs. Grantham," he stammered, enraged and confounded at this unexpected repulse, "surely you must have seen, you must have known—the devotion of years—"

Either inability to proceed, or an expression in her face, restrained him here.

"Do not say what cannot be unsaid or forgotten. It will be best for both of us. Clair and I have been very happy during our visit. If you wish to drive us away—"

"No, no!" he cried; "you are cruel to make the suggestion. I do not deserve such a return. My mother would look upon it as an affront; and Charlotte— you love Charlotte—"

He hardly knew what to say in his confusion; but he felt it would be quite fatal to his hopes if he lost his present hold upon her.

"You do not deserve such a return," she said; "and not for worlds would I wound your mother's feelings or yours. It was only an hour ago that I promised Charlotte not to curtail my visit; and I will promise you, if you will engage not to reopen the subject. Let us forget what has passed. Shall we exchange promises?"

She held out her hand, and he deluded himself into the belief that he saw signs of softening in her face. As he took her hand his native cunning and coolness returned to him, and he was more than ever determined that she should not slip from him. He would be her master yet, and she should pay for her treatment of him. Even as he held her hand in his, the skeleton of a scheme to force her compliance presented itself to his mind, fertile in schemes and snares.

"I am almost inclined to be jealous of dear Clair," he said, in a plaintive tone, "for she seems to stand in the way of my happiness."

"You must not say that. If it were not for her, I might not be living this day. Through her, I saw my duty clear before me. I live only for her and for her happiness. It is an understanding, then?"

"Yes," he said, "it is an understanding. Excuse me now; I will go and give these flowers to Charlotte."

But he did nothing of the kind. He walked away, and when he was sure that no one saw him he tore the posy to pieces, and trod savagely upon the fragments, stamping at the same time upon every living thing beneath him that caught his eye. Such acts of destruction and cruelty always afforded him satisfaction, and after a few minutes so occupied he devoted himself more calmly to the difficulties of his position. Gradually a scheme formed itself in his mind, and he smiled at the thought that it would lead him to victory. He recalled the words Mrs. Grantham had spoken:

"The love of her child is a heavenly consolation to her, and she has consecrated her life to the brat. She lives only for Clair's happiness. If I prove to her how that happiness is imperiled, and that her infernal consecration will land her in the gutter .... Yes, I see my way; I see my way!"

But he saw not the Nemesis that was following his footsteps, born of a base action he had committed without ruth or remorse. He thought it was dead and buried, and that a woman he had wronged—not the only one—was happily lost to him, if not to the world. Neither did he bestow a thought upon Robert Grantham, nor upon the double deceit he had practiced upon husband and wife. In fancied security he paced a secluded path, meditating upon the new lie which would bring Mrs. Grantham to her knees, for the sake of the child she loved so well.

CHAPTER XI.

Little Prue.

Who Roxy was, what was his occupation, and whether he lived in a bygone age or was living at the present day, are matters which are not pertinent to our story, the course of which brings us, in a remote and indirect manner, to the knowledge that such a being once existed, or exists now. That he was responsible for the miserable dozen tenements known as "Roxy's Rents" may be accepted, as may be also the undoubted reason for his giving them the eccentric name they bore; the rents of the hovels he erected being lawfully his, if he could find tenants to occupy them.

A stranger to the wretched ways of life of thousands upon thousands of poor people in such a city as London might reasonably have doubted the wisdom of spending money in the erection of such hovels; but Roxy knew what he was about when he went into the speculation. A comprehensive knowledge of humanity's outcasts had taught him that the more dismal and wretched the habitations, the more likely it was that there would be numerous applicants for the shelter they afforded; and his wisdom was proved by the result, not a room in Roxy's Rents ever being empty longer than a day or two. The narrow blind alley lined by the hovels, half a dozen on each side, may be found to-day in all its desolation or wretchedness in the south of London, by any person with a leaning to such explorations. It is well known to the police, who seldom have occasion to go there, because, strangely enough, it is chiefly tenanted by people who work hard for a living, often without obtaining it.

Roxy himself, or his agent, who collects the rents regularly every Saturday night from eight o'clock till past midnight, is very particular in his choice of tenants, which he is able to be by reason of the delectable tenements being in demand. There are numbers of landlords in more favored localities who would like to stand in Roxy's shoes in this respect. The alley is some eight feet wide, and its one architectural embellishment is a kind of hood at its entrance, the only use of which is to deepen its darkness by day and night. There is no public lamp in Roxy's Rents, nor near it in the street, very little wider than the alley, in which it forms a slit; therefore the darkness is very decided in its character on foggy days and moonless nights. This has never been a subject of complaint on the part of the residents or the parish authorities—officers who, as a rule, have an objection to stir up muddy waters: by which inaction they show their respect for an ancient proverb, the vulgar version of which is, "Let sleeping dogs lie." To one of the hovels in Roxy's Rents the course of our story takes us.

The room is on the ground floor, the time is night, the persons in it are a woman and her child. The woman's name is Flower; the name of her child, a girl of eight or nine, is Prue, generally called "Little Prue." The apartment is used for every kind of living purpose—working, cooking, eating, and sleeping, It is furnished with an ordinary stove, one bed on the floor in a corner (a bedstead being a luxury beyond the means of the family), two wooden chairs, a child's low chair, the seat of which once was cane but now is hollow, a deal table, a few kitchen utensils, and very little else. On the mantelshelf are two or three cracked cups and saucers, a penny, and a much-faded photograph of two young women, with, their arms round each other's waists. There is a family likeness in their faces, and one bears a faint resemblance to Mrs. Flower. The paper on the walls hangs loose, and the walls themselves reek with moisture; the plaster on the ceiling has dropped in places, and bare rafters are visible. Not a palatial abode, but the Flowers have lived there for years, and it forms their Home—a mocking parody on a time-honored song. Mrs. Flower is standing at the table, ironing clothes. She takes in washing when she can get it to do, having but few garments of her own to wash.

Mrs. Flower was working with a will, putting her whole soul into the iron. The apartment was chiefly in shadow, the only light being that from one tallow dip, twelve to the pound. The candle was on the table, being necessary for the woman's work, and its rays did not reach Little Prue, who sat in the low hollow-seated chair by the bed. Mrs. Flower enlivened her toil by singing, or rather humming with bated breath, a most lugubrious air for which she was famous in her maiden days, but then it used to be given forth with more spirit than she put into it now. Occasionally she turned to her child, who was sitting quite still with her eyes closed. There was a faint sickly smell of scorching in the room, proceeding from a wisp of carpet on the floor before the fire, upon which Mrs. Flower tested her hot irons. It had served this purpose so long that it was scorched almost to tinder. Presently the woman broke off in her melancholy singing, and called softly:

"Prue!" No answer coming, she called again, "Prue!"

"Yes, mother," said the child, opening her eyes. Her voice was weak, as might have been expected from a child with a face so pale and limbs so thin.

"I thought you were asleep, Prue."

"So I was, mother. Why didn't you let me be?"

"Dreaming of things?"

"Oh, of sech things, mother! I was 'aving a feast of sheep's trotters." Mrs. Flower sighed. "There was a 'ole pile of 'em, and the 'ot pie man was giving pies away. I was just reaching out my 'and for one."

"Never mind, never mind," said Mrs. Flower, rather fretfully. "You talk as if I could get blood out of a stone."

"Do I, mother? I didn't know. I _am_ 'ungry!"

"What's the use of worriting? Didn't I promise you should have some supper? I'm going to ask Mrs. Fry to pay me for the washing when I take it home. I do hope she won't say there's anything missing. She always does; and when I ask her to look over the things again, she sends word she can't till the morning. That's how she puts me off time after time; but I'll be extra particular to-night. Three dozen at one and nine—that's five and three. She don't often give out so much; that's luck for us, Prue."

"I say, mother?"

"Well?"

"D'yer think father'll come 'ome? I 'ope he won't."

"He won't come home while he's got a copper in his pocket, that you may depend on. Go to sleep again, child, till I've finished."

But Little Prue, now wide awake, made no attempt to obey. Rising to her feet, she stealthily drew one of the large wooden chairs to the mantelshelf, and, mounting, craned her neck. The shelf was high, and Prue was a very small child. It was only by tiptoeing, and running the danger of tumbling into the fire, that she ascertained what she wished to know. Stepping down like a cat, she crept to her mother's side.

"There's a penny on the mantelpiece, mother."

"Don't worry; how can I get on with my work if you do? It's father's penny, for his supper beer; he put it there before he went out, so that he couldn't spend it till he came home." Aside she said, with a sidelong look of pity at Prue, "I daren't touch it!"

"I'm so 'ungry, mother!" pleaded Prue, plucking her mother's gown. "My inside's grinding away like one o'clock."

Mrs. Flower was seized with a fit of irresolution, and she muttered, "If I look sharp, I shall be back with the washing money before he comes in." Stepping quickly to the fireplace, she took the penny from the mantel, and thrust it into Prue's hand. "There; go and get a penn'orth of peas-pudding."

"Oh, mother, mother!" cried Little Prue joyfully, and was running out, when the door was blocked by the form of her father, who had returned sooner than he was expected.

Mr. Flower was slightly intoxicated—his normal state. However much he drank, he never got beyond a certain stage of drunkenness; by reason, probably, of his being so thoroughly seasoned.

"Hallo, hallo!" he cried, grasping his little girl by the shoulder. "Is the house on fire? Where are _you_ off to in such a hurry?"

"Nowhere, father," replied Prue, slipping her hand with the penny in it behind her back.

"Nowhere, eh? You're in a precious pelt to get there. What have you got in your hand?"

"Nothink, father!"

"Nothink, father!" he mocked, eyeing Prue with something more than suspicion.

"No, father. Wish I may die if I 'ave!"

Without more ado, Mr. Flower seized the little hand and, wresting the tightly-clenched fingers open, extracted the penny. Looking toward the mantelshelf, he said:

"Stealing my money, eh, you young rat? Who learnt you to tell lies?"

"You did!" replied Mrs. Flower, stepping between them. She had finished her washing, and was putting it together while this scene was proceeding. "You did, you drunken vagabond!"

"You shut up! As for you," he said, throwing Prue violently on the bed; "you stop where you are, or I'll break every bone in your body!"

"Lay a finger on her," cried Mrs. Flower fiercely, "and I'll throw the iron at your head! Don't mind him, Prue; I'll soon be back."

"Ah, you'd better!" said Mr. Flower, with a brutal laugh at his wife, who was looking at him in anger. "What are you staring at?"

"At you."

"Well, and what do you make of me?"

"What I've made of you ever since the day I married you."

"For better or worse, eh?"

"For worse, every minute of my life," she retorted. "I wonder why the Lord allows some people to live."

"Here, that's enough of your mag, with your Lord and your Lord! What's your Lord done for me? Off you go, now!"

But Mrs. Flower was not so easily disposed of.

"Have you brought home any money?" she asked.

"Money! How should I get money?"

"Why work for it, like other men, you—" She repressed herself, and, with a flaming face, arranged the clothes she had washed.

"Work for it!" he cried, with a laugh, and immediately afterward turned savage. "Well, ain't I willing?"

"Yes, you show yourself willing," said Mrs. Flower, bitterly; "hanging round public-houses, and loafing from morning to night!"

"Think I'm going to work for a tanner an hour?" demanded Mr. Flower. "Not me! I'll have my rights, I will!"

"While we starve!"

"Starve! When you can get washing to do, and live on the fat of the land! If I was a woman, I'd rejoice in such clean work."

"And don't I do it? Haven't I sat up night after night, wearing my fingers to the bone for you?"

"For me? Oh, oh! I like that!"

"Yes, for you," repeated Mrs. Flower, thoroughly roused. "And what's the good of it all? You drink away every penny I earn, you sot; and you call yourself a man!"

"I'll call you something, if you don't cut your stick! I wonder what I married you for?"

"I'll tell you. You married me to make me work for you; and you're not the only one that speaks soft to a woman till he's got her in his clutches. There ought to be a law for such as you."

"Law! Talk of what you understand. There was your sister Martha. Ah, she was a girl! Such eyes—such skin—such lips!" He smacked his own, in his desire to further aggravate her. "I was real nuts on her; and I'd have had her instead of you, if she hadn't took up with a swell. I hope she's found out her mistake by this time."

"I dare say she has. We all do, whether we're married or not." She turned to Little Prue, who sat dumb during the scene, which presented no features of novelty to her; from her earliest remembrance she had been a witness of such. "I shan't be gone long," she whispered, kissing the child, "and then you shall have some supper."

"Mind you get the money for the washing, and bring it straight home!"— called Mr. Flower after her as she left the room. "Selfish cat!" He slammed the door to. "Never thinks of anyone but herself—never thinks of me! What are you sniveling at?" Prue, now that her mother had gone, began to cry. "Come here; I've got something to say to you. Ain't I your father?"

"Yes, father."

"And a good father?"

"Yes, father."

"And a kind father?"

"Yes, father."

"Very well, then. How old are you?"

"I don't know, father."

"You don't know, father! You're old enough to get your own living, and here you are passing your days in idleness and plenty. D'you see these!" He pulled some boxes of matches from his pocket.

"Yes, father."

"What are they?"

"Matches, father."

"Count 'em. D'you hear me? Count 'em." The child was reeling, and he shook her straight. "Count 'em."

"One—two—three—four—five—six."

"Six it is. Now, you've got to go out with these six boxes of matches, and bring home tenpence for 'em. How are you going to do it, eh?"

"I don't know, father."

"Don't give me any more of your don't knows. You've got no more sense than your mother; but I'm not going to let you grow up as idle and selfish as she is—not if I know it, I ain't. Stop your blubbering, and listen to me. You go to Charing Cross Station, you do, where all the lights are, and where everybody's happy. What are you shaking your head for?"

"I don't know—I mean, I can't find my way, father."

"I shall have to take you there; I'm only fit to be a slave. There you'll stand, with the lights shining on you. That'll be nice, won't it?"

"Yes, father."

"Nice and warm; and you get it for nothing, all for nothing. There's a treat I'm giving you! You stand in the gutter, mind that; and you ain't to look happy and bright. You're to try all you know to look miserable and hungry. Do you hear?"

"I'll try to, father."

"Ah, you'd better, or it'll be the worse for you! When an old gent or an old lady gives you a penny, don't you offer 'em a box; there's a lot of mean beasts that'd take it. You hold the boxes tight, and you bring me back not less than a bob for the six—not less than a bob, mind!"

"Yes, father."

"Here, I'll give you a lesson. Blest if we don't have a rehearsal! Stand there, in the gutter, and look miserable. I'm a gent. Hold out your hand. 'Here's a penny for you, little girl.' Take it—quick! and hold on tight to the matches. The gent goes away. I'm an old lady. 'My poor child, what brings you out at such an hour?' What do you say to the kind old lady?"

"Father sent me out, please; and told me to stand in the gutter—"

"Shut up! You're a born fool! What you say is this. Just you repeat after me. 'Kind lady—'"

"'Kind lady!'"

"'Father's dead—'"

"'Father's dead!'"

"'And mother's laying ill of a fever—'"

"'And mother's laying ill of a fever!'"

"'And baby's dying—'"

"'And baby's dying!'"

"''Cause we ain't had nothing to eat since yesterday—'"

"''Cause we ain't 'ad nothink to eat since yesterday!'"

"That's more like it. And then you can begin to cry. Have you got that in your head?"

"Yes, father."

"Come along, then, and step out. I'll keep my eye on you to see how you do it."

Taking Little Prue by the hand, he led her out of Roxy's Rents into the wider thoroughfares, to play her part in the sad drama of poverty that runs its everlasting course from year's end to year's end in this City of Unrest.

CHAPTER XII.

"Drip-Drip-Drip!"

As they issued from the hooded portal of Roxy's Rents, a woe-stricken woman approached the alley, and looked wearily around. Dark as was the night, and though years had passed since she had visited the locality, she had found her way without inquiry; but her steps faltered at the entrance to the narrow court, and her manner was that of one who was uncertain of the errand she had undertaken. To resolve her doubts, she accosted a young girl about to pass her:

"This is Roxy's Rents, isn't it?"

"Yes," replied the girl.

"Can you tell me if Mrs. Flower lives here?"

"Yes, the last house but one on the right; front room, ground floor."

"Is she at home, do you know?"

"I don't know."

"Thank you."

The girl went her way, singing; she was in her spring. The woman entered the alley, sighing; winter had come upon her too soon. When she arrived at the last house but one on the right, she seemed to be glad to see the glimmering of a light through the torn blind on the front window. The street door stood open, and she stepped into the dark passage, and paused before the door of the room in which Mrs. Flower lived.

"Janey!" she called, and listened for the answer. None reaching her ear, she entered without further ceremony. The candle, which Mr. Flower had inadvertently left alight, was burnt nearly to its socket, and the woman shivered as she noted the unmistakable signs of privation in the room.

"It _is_ Janey's place, I suppose!" she said, and looking toward the mantelshelf, saw there the faded photograph of herself and sister. "Yes, it's all right." She took down the photograph, and gazed at it with a curl of her lip as rueful as it was bitter. "Here we are together, Janey and me, before ... ." A shudder served to complete the sentence. "How well I remember the day this was taken! We had a week at the seaside, and stood together on the sands, as happy as birds. The sun was shining, the children were playing and laughing. If I had known—if I had known! I never see children laughing now, and I sometimes wonder if the sun ever comes out. I was good-looking then, and nicely dressed, and no one could say anything against me. But what's the use of thinking about it? Thinking won't alter it."

She had contracted a habit of speaking to herself, and was scarcely conscious that she was uttering audible words.

"I don't mean to stand it long," she said presently. "I've come to London for something, and if he doesn't do what he ought to, I'll put an end to it. As I'm a living woman, I'll put an end to it! I don't care much which way it is. I've nothing to live for now!"

She sat down and covered her face with her hands; the candle had been spluttering and, being now at its last gasp, went out. The woman was left in darkness. It suited her mood. The sound of water slowly dropping outside attracted her attention. She removed her hands from her face, and listened; as she listened she followed the rhythm with the sound of her voice.

"Drip, drip drip! Drip, drip, drip!"

The pattering of the drops and her accompaniment fascinated her.

"Drip, drip, drip!" she continued to murmur, and did not stop till another sound diverted her attention. The door of the room was sharply opened, and Mrs. Flower entered. The woman stirred in her chair.

"Is that you, Prue?" asked Mrs. Flower. "Stop a minute; I'll get a light."

"No," replied the woman, "it isn't Prue."

"My God!" cried Mrs. Flower, "whose voice is that?"

She groped for the end of a candle, and lit it; holding it up, she looked at her visitor, who had risen, and was facing her.

"Martha!"

"Yes, Janey, it's me. You're not glad to see me, I dare say, after all these years."

"How can you say that? How long have you been here, and where's Prue?"

"I've been here—I don't know how long, and there was no one in the room when I came in. Who's Prue?"

"My little girl. Where can she have got to? I forgot, Janey. I didn't have a baby when—" She paused.

"Finish it," said Martha. "When I ran away and disgraced myself."

"O Martha!" said Mrs. Fowler, throwing her arms round her sister and kissing her, "don't think I'm hard on you. God knows I've no call to be hard on anyone, least of all on you. We all make mistakes."

"And have got to pay for them. Thank you for your welcome, Janey; it's more than I deserve."

"You're my sister, and I love you, Martha. Sit down, sit down, and tell me everything. How often I've wondered what had become of you! But I'm worried about Prue. I left her here with her father when I went out."

"Your husband's alive. That's a comfort."

"Is it? You wouldn't say so if he was yours. I suppose he's taken her into the streets with him. He's done it before, and got her to beg for him, the brute! It's no use my going out to find her; I shouldn't know where to look."

"That tells a tale, and I am sorry for you, Janey. I mightn't have come if I'd known; but I'd nowhere else to go to."

106

"Of course you came here. What a time it is since we saw each other!"

"We haven't improved much, either of us," said Martha. "I was hoping you were better off."

"I might have been if my husband was a man. The truth must be told: I couldn't be worse off than I am, I left my Prue hungry, and promised her some supper. I take in washing, Martha, and there was five shillings due to me, but the woman wouldn't pay me to-night; I've got to wait till to-morrow, so Prue will have to go to sleep on an empty stomach. It's hard lines on a sickly child, but what can I do?"

"I can't assist you, Janey. I've spent my last penny."

"There's no help for it, then; we're in the same boat. But tell me where you've been all these years."

"In Manchester. It's a puzzle to me how I got here, but I made up my mind to come to London, to try and screw something out of the man who took me away from home. I've got his address, and I went to his house this afternoon. He was away in the country, they told me, but I couldn't get them to tell me where. There was a man saw me standing at his door after they'd shut it in my face, and he came up and asked if he could do anything for me, and whether I would mind telling him what I wanted with Mr. Fox-Cordery, for that's the name of the villain that deceived me, but I said it was no business of his, and I walked away, and left him looking after me. I wandered about till it was dark, and then I thought I'd come and ask you to let me sleep here to-night. Must I turn out?"

"How can you ask such a thing? You're welcome to stop if you don't mind. This is the only room we've got, and I can't give you anything to eat because the cupboard's as empty as my pocket."

"Oh, I'm used to that! Your heart isn't changed, Janey."

"I couldn't be hard to you if I tried; and I'm not going to try. In Manchester you've been? You disappeared so suddenly and mysteriously—"

"Yes, yes; but we were carrying on together long before I went away. He wanted to get me out of London, away from him, you know: he was tired of me, and I wasn't in the best of tempers; he got frightened a bit, I think, because I said if he threw me over I'd have him up at the police court when my baby was born. He's a very respectable man—oh, very respectable!—and looks as soft and speaks as soft as if butter wouldn't melt in his mouth. But he's clever, and cunning, and sly, for all that, and he talked me over. I was to go away from London, and he was to allow me so much a week. He did for a little while, and sent it on to me in Manchester. Janey, when he first pretended to get fond of me he promised to marry me."

"Yes, they all do that, and women are fools enough to believe em."

"I was, and I used to remind him of his promise. That was while I was in London. When I was in Manchester he thought himself safe. Then my baby came, and it cost him a little. I had to write to him for every shilling almost, and he'd send me a postal order without a word of writing to say who it came from. That made me wild, and I wrote and said if he didn't write me proper letters I'd come back to London and worry his life out of him. That pulled him up, and he did write, but he never signed his name. He just put 'F.' at the bottom of his letters; I've got them in my pocket, every one of them. Well, then I got a situation as a shop-woman—they didn't know I had a baby, and I didn't tell them, you may be sure—and I put by a shilling or two. It was wanted, because his money dropped off. I lost my situation, and then I frightened him into coming to Manchester to see me. He was as soft and smooth as ever, and he swore to me that I should never want; he took his oath on it, and I told him if he didn't keep it I'd make it hot for him. Janey, you don't know the promises that man made to me when we first came together; it was a long time before I could bring myself to like him, but he spoke so fair that at last I gave way. And he played me false, after all. Don't think that I wanted to sponge on him; if I could have got my own living in an honest way. —and I never intend to get it any other way; I'm not thoroughly bad, Janey— I wouldn't have troubled him; but I couldn't. I have been in such misery, that if it had not been for my child I should have made away with myself long ago; but nothing keeps me back now. I have lost my child; it was buried by the parish."

"Hush, Martha, hush!"

"It's no use talking to me, Janey. I can't live this life any longer; and if the man that's brought me to it won't help me, I've made up my mind what to do. Nothing can change it—nothing. Look at me; I've hardly a rag to my back. It's a rosy look-out, to-morrow is. If I had decent clothes and a pound in my pocket, I might get into service; but who'd take me as I am?"

"You are changed from what you were, Martha; you used to be as merry as a lark."

"The lark's taken out of me long ago, and you haven't much of it left in you that I can see. I don't know that you're any better off than me, though you _are_ a respectable married woman; you've had to pay for your respectability. Much comfort it brings you, according to your own reckoning! What water is that dripping outside?"

She asked this question in the dark; the candle had gone out, and Mrs.

Flower had no more.

"The water-butt leaks."

"Drip, drip, drip—and then it becomes a large pool—I see it spreading out —large enough to drown one's self in!"

"Martha!"

"Which would be best, Janey? That or what I shall be forced into if no one helps me? Supposing I'm alive! There it goes—drip, drip, drip! It might be drops of blood. There isn't a sheet of water I've seen since my child died that hasn't seemed to draw me to it, that hasn't whispered, 'Come, and end it!' When you wake up of a morning sometimes, aren't you sorry?"

"I am, God help me!"

"You've had a long sleep, and you've been happy; and you wake up—to this! Wouldn't it be better never to wake up? Drip, drip, drip! It's singing 'Come, come, come!' It drips just to that tune." She began to sing softly, with a pause between each word, to keep time to the water, "Come—come—come! Let me alone, Janey; don't lay hands on me. I'm all right for a day or two—I won't say for how much longer. I'll try and get some sleep."

CHAPTER XIII.

In which Rathbeal makes a winning Move.

On this same day Rathbeal had met with adventures. There was a coffee shop in his neighborhood to which he was in the habit of going, two or three times a week, to have a cup of coffee and play a game of chess with the hoary proprietor.

It belonged to a class of shops which once were a favorite resort for working people, but are now fast dying out; they are only to be found in second-class neighborhoods, and seem, as it were, to be striving to keep themselves out of sight, with a painful consciousness that they are relics of a bygone age, and have no business to be in existence. It cannot be said that they die hard, for there is a patient and sad resignation in their appearance, which in its humbleness and abasement is almost pathetic. The interior of these shops is as shabby and uninviting as their exterior. There are the narrow boxes which cramp the legs to sit in, the tables are bare of covering, the knives and forks are of ancient fashion, the crockery is in its last stage, and the once brilliant luster of the dominoes has quite disappeared, double one especially looking up with two hollow dead white eyes which cannot but have an inexpressibly depressing influence upon the players. The draughts and chessmen with their one wooden board are in a like condition of decay, and the games played thereon are the reverse of lively. There is another peculiarity which forces itself upon the attention. All the newspapers are old, some dating back several weeks, and they are allowed to lie about till they are in a condition so disgraceful that they are fit for nothing but lighting fires. These newspapers are never bought on the day of issue, but considerably later on, at less than a quarter their original price. Thus it was that in the coffee shop to which Rathbeal was in the habit of resorting there were always to be found two or three copies of the _Times_, of dates varying from one to two months ago.

On the day in question, Rathbeal, while the hoary proprietor was fetching the chessmen and board, happened to take up one of these sheets and run his eyes down the columns. It was not news he was glancing at, but advertisements, and he was conning the first page of the newspaper. When the proprietor of the shop took his seat opposite to him and arranged his men, Rathbeal, folding the paper neatly, laid it beside him on the table. Then he proceeded to place his warriors, and the game was commenced. The proprietor was a slow player, Rathbeal moved very quickly; thus it was that he had plenty of leisure to glance from time to time at the newspaper by his side. "Check," he called, and turned his eyes upon the paper. A sudden color flushed into his face, caused by an advertisement he had up to this time overlooked. This was what he read:

> If Mr. Robert Grantham, born in Leamington, Warwickshire, will call upon Messrs. Paxton and Freshfield, solicitors, Bedford Row, London, he will hear of something to his advantage.

Rising hastily, he upset the chessboard. The proprietor looked up in surprise.

"Your game," said Rathbeal, and then consulted the date of the newspaper. It was nearly seven weeks old. Permission being given to him to make a cutting from the paper, he cut out the advertisement very neatly, and asked the proprietor whether he had a London Directory in the shop.

"I have one," said the proprietor, "but it is twelve years old."

"That will do," said Rathbeal. "Lawyers are rocks."

Turning over the pages of the Directory, he found the number in Bedford Row at which Paxton and Freshfield carried on their practice. Wishing the proprietor good-day, he left the shop, and went straight to Robert Grantham's lodging. Grantham was at home.

"I have something to ask you, Robert," he said, without beating about the bush. "Were you born in Leamington?"

"Yes," replied Grantham.

"Leamington in Warwickshire?"

"Yes."

"Then this concerns you," said Rathbeal, and handed him the cutting.

The expression on Robert Grantham's face was not one of pleasure; to be thus publicly advertised for seemed to cause him discomfort. He read the advertisement, and offered no remark upon it.

"It was by chance," said Rathbeal, "using your own term, for I do not admit that chance is a factor in our lives, that I came across it. The paper I cut it from is nearly two months old. What are you going to do about it?"

"Nothing," said Grantham.

"Something to your advantage, it says. That sounds like money. You cannot afford to neglect it, Robert."

"I would rather have nothing to do with it."

"Gently, friend. How much coin have you in your pocket at the present moment?"

"Two small silver pieces and a few pennies. To be exact, one shilling and tenpence."

"Your rent is due to-morrow."

"I shall earn it."

"Do not be too sure. If this advertisement means money for you, it becomes your duty to claim it."

"How so?"

"Remember the penance you imposed upon yourself. You would spend for your own necessities only what was requisite for the plainest food; any money you had remaining should be devoted to the children of misery. You have nobly carried out your resolution. Do you consider you have atoned for the sins and errors of the past?"

"I could not atone for them if I lived twice my allotted span."

"Then the right is not yours to throw away this money. It belongs, not to you, but to the poor, whose sufferings it would alleviate. Neglect of the opportunity which now presents itself would become a crime. And why do you desire to let the matter rest? To save yourself a possible personal annoyance, you shrink from publicity; you tremble at the idea that some old friend or acquaintance may learn that you still live. I did not think you capable of such weakness."

"I am reproved, Rathbeal; but still I would rather not appear in the matter until the last moment, until it is certain that my appearance is necessary, and would benefit others. Will you take this office of friendship upon yourself, and make inquiries for me at the lawyer's?"

"Willingly, if you will give me full powers. I must be prepared to show that I am acting for you."

"Draw up a paper, Rathbeal. I will sign whatever you write."

In his neat handwriting Rathbeal drew out something in the shape of a power of attorney, which Robert Grantham signed. Before he went upon his mission Rathbeal made an appointment to meet Grantham at nine o'clock that night; the appointment would have been made for an earlier hour, but Grantham had some copying to finish and deliver, and the work could not be neglected.

When Rathbeal arrived at the offices of Paxton and Freshfield he asked to see one of the principals, and he heard a clerk tell another to see if Mr. Dixon was in. Mr. Dixon was not in, but Mr. Paxton was, and would see Mr. Rathbeal.

"I have come about this advertisement," he said, showing the cutting to an old gentleman wearing gold spectacles.

Mr. Paxton glanced at the advertisement, and said:

"Our partner, Mr. Dixon, has taken it in hand; he will return at four o'clock."

"I will wait for him," said Rathbeal, "but meanwhile you can perhaps give me some information concerning it."

"I know very little about it," said the lawyer, cautiously. "Mr. Dixon is in possession of the full particulars. You are not Mr. Grantham?" He referred to the card Rathbeal had sent in.

"No, I am Mr. Grantham's friend and agent. I have authority to act for him." He produced the document Grantham had signed. "It is drawn out and signed to-day, you see."

"I see. How is it that so long a time has elapsed before answering the advertisement?"

"It only came to Mr. Grantham's knowledge a couple of hours ago. Would you object to inform me whether it is really something to his advantage, whether it means money?"

"There is a small legacy left to Mr. Grantham, I believe, which he can obtain if the proofs are clear."

A clerk knocked at the door, and entered. "Mr. Dixon has come in, sir."

"Show this gentleman to his room."

Being introduced to Mr. Dixon, Rathbeal opened up his business, and observed signs of agitation in John Dixon's face, which he construed unfavorably. With the signed document before him—which he examined, Rathbeal thought, with suspicious attention—John Dixon schooled himself presently to a more strictly professional method, but he did not immediately make any observation.

"The document is genuine, sir," said Rathbeal. "It was signed in my presence."

"Upon that point," said John Dixon, with studious brows, "I must be quite certain. You are a stranger to me, and your name is strange; and you bring me startling news, Mr. Rathbeal. Why did not Mr. Grantham come himself? Are you aware that it is believed by his friends that he is dead?"

"I know that it was his wish to be thought so, and I am acquainted with his reasons for a course of conduct which, without proper explanation, must be viewed with mistrust. As to the trouble I am taking, it is, I assure you, sir, not actuated by selfish motives. He has a strong disinclination to appear personally in the matter, and his motives could only be disclosed to friends in whom he has the most thorough confidence. I can satisfy you as to my respectability—"

"I throw no doubt upon it, Mr. Rathbeal: you do not seem to understand that the intervention of a second party is quite useless. The principal must appear himself."

"I accept your word, sir, but I would ask you whether the affair could not be conducted confidentially—without publicity, I mean. I have learnt that a small legacy has been left to Mr. Grantham. However small it is, it will be of great value to him: he is very poor, as I am myself."

John Dixon did a singular thing here. Motioning Rathbeal not to proceed at present, he arranged the papers on his table, put others in a desk, which he locked, opened a shut-up washstand and laved his hands, brushed his hair, put on his hat, and then asked Rathbeal to give him the favor of his company in his private chambers, which were situated in Craven Street, Strand. Rathbeal consenting, they walked together from the office, and John Dixon called a cab, in which they rode to Craven Street. On the road Rathbeal would have continued to speak of the mission he had undertaken, but John Dixon said, "Wait till we get to my rooms; these confounded wheels make conversation difficult." His voice, as he made this observation, was entirely different from the professional voice he had adopted in the office; there was a frank heartiness in it which attracted Rathbeal favorably, and he deferred to his companion's wish and said nothing more till they arrived at Craven Street.

"Sit down, Mr. Rathbeal," said John Dixon. "Let me offer you a cigar. Now we can speak openly; I am no longer a lawyer; I am Robert Grantham's friend. You look surprised. I have a very close interest in the news you have brought me, and if you have spoken the truth—pardon me for saying this; I am justified by the nature of the circumstances—I may be able to serve him, and shall be glad to do so. If I understand aright, you and he are intimate friends."

"We have been intimate friends for years. There is no man living for whom I have a greater affection."

"You state that the signature to the document empowering you to act for him is in his handwriting."

"I saw him write it."

"This very day?"

"This very day. The date is on the paper."

"Could you take me to him?"

"I could, but I would not do so without his permission."

"We are both on guard, as it were, Mr. Rathbeal. I was Robert Grantham's schoolfellow."

"That is a piece of news," said Rathbeal, and added significantly, "He had other schoolfellows."

"Shall we say one especially?"

"Yes, we will say that."

"Whose name you know?"

"Whose name I know."

"I am tempted to make a curious proposition to you, which if you accede to, and it turns out successful, may satisfy each of us that we may work together on behalf of one whose career has been unfortunate and unhappy."

"Make your proposition, sir."

"One other of Robert Grantham's schoolfellows has been referred to. We will each write down his name on separate pieces of paper, which we will exchange. If the name is the same, we can proceed with our conversation with less reserve."

"I agree, sir," said Rathbeal, and wrote the name that was in his mind.

John Dixon did the same, and when they exchanged papers they saw that the name they had penciled was "Fox-Cordery."

"Could we exchange opinions of this gentleman on the same plan?" asked John Dixon.

"I will give you mine, sir, byword of mouth. The gentleman, as you call him, is a reptile in human shape. To touch his hand in friendship is a degradation."

"The terms are strong, but he has proved deserving of them. The peculiar circumstances of my connection with him would have made the expression of my opinion more temperate. You must be aware of the imperative necessity of carrying the disclosure of the existence of Robert Grantham to other ears, even though he persists in keeping himself in concealment."

"No, sir, I am aware of no such necessity," said Rathbeal. "For reasons best known to himself, Mr. Fox-Cordery desired the death of Mr. Grantham. Some short time since, disturbed probably by something that had come to his ears, he paid me a visit to assure himself that Mr. Grantham was not of this world. I refused to betray the confidence reposed in me by my friend, and Mr. Fox-Cordery went away no wiser, for any information he received from me, than he came."

"Are you quite honest," said John Dixon rather sternly, "in saying that you are not aware of the necessity for Mr. Grantham making his existence known to certain persons?"

"Perfectly honest, sir. Mr. Grantham is alone in the world; no one has the least claim upon him, and whatever judgment you may pass upon him, he has a distinct right to do as he pleases with himself and his identity."

"Have you no thought for his wife and child?" asked John Dixon. "Do you really maintain that a husband and a father has the right to assist by his own premeditated action in the lie that his wife is a widow and his child an orphan?"

"I should be sorry to maintain an assumption so monstrous. We cannot assist each other by playing at cross-purposes, which is what we appear to be doing. Mr. Grantham, I repeat, is alone in the world. He has no wife and child."

"He has no wife and child!" exclaimed John Dixon, in amazement.

"Unhappily, he has lost them, and it is the distressing circumstances of this sad loss that has made him what he is—an outcast on the face of the earth. As we have gone so far, sir, I may tell you that Mr. Grantham has no secrets from me. He has revealed to me all the sorrowful circumstances of his life, and he has drained the bitter cup of agony and remorse. I trust to you, sir, to keep this confidence sacred. You have wrung it out of me, and it must go no farther. If Mr. Grantham consents to see you, and if then he confides to you what he has confided to me, you will receive from him a full verification of my statements. Will you now, sir, give me the particulars of the legacy that has been left to him?"

It was impossible for John Dixon to doubt that Rathbeal was speaking without guile or deceit. His manly, sympathetic voice, the frankness of his manner, and his honest look carried conviction with them.

"We will speak of the legacy presently," he said. "There is a mystery here which must first be cleared up. From whom did you receive the information that Mr. Robert Grantham's wife and child were dead?"

"From his own lips."

"How did he obtain the information?"

"It came through Mr. Fox-Cordery."

116

"Do you tell me this seriously," asked John Dixon, pale with excitement, "or are you inventing a fantastic and horrible tale for some purpose of your own?"

"I have no purpose of my own to serve," replied Rathbeal. "I am here to serve a noble and suffering man, who erred grievously in years gone by, and who is now passing his life in the work of expiation. Your words, your manner, point to a mystery indeed—a mystery it is out of my power to pierce. I scarcely know what to say, what to think. You could not demand from me a sacrifice I would be unwilling to make if I could assist in bringing comfort to my friend's heart. Trust me, sir; I am worthy of trust. Do not speak to me in metaphor; but explain to me the meaning of words I cannot at present understand."

During the last few moments there had dawned upon John Dixon a light in which Mr. Fox-Cordery's villainous duplicity was to some extent made clear, and he resolved to avail himself of Rathbeal's assistance to bring him to justice. A husband who believed that those he loved were in their grave, a wife who believed herself widowed, a child who believed she was an orphan —the figures of these three wronged beings rose before him, and appealed to him to take up their cause and bring the truth to light.

"If I were to tell you," he said slowly, "that I have this day written to Robert Grantham's wife, informing her of the legacy left to her husband, and asking for her instructions thereon, what would you say?"

Hitherto Rathbeal had preserved his calmness, but it was his turn now to exhibit agitation.

"You have written to Robert Grantham's wife!" he exclaimed. "To Robert Grantham's wife, who is in her grave!"

"She lives," said John Dixon, "and is now, with her child, in Mr. Fox-Cordery's house."

"The child's name, Clair?"

"The child's name, Clair," said John Dixon. "The time for concealment is over; plain-speaking is now the order of the day, and Justice our watchword. Tell me all you know; you shall receive a like confidence from me."

Thereupon the men related to each other all they knew of husband, wife, and child; and when their stories were told Mr. Fox-Cordery's wiles were fully exposed. Uncertain on the spur of the moment what action it was advisable to take, they pledged each other to secrecy for two days, by which time they would have devised a plan to unmask the traitor. Their reason for resolving not to communicate their discoveries immediately to Robert

Grantham was that they feared he would do some rash action which would put Mr. Fox-Cordery on his guard, and give him an opportunity to crawl out of the net he had woven around these innocent beings, and which now was closing round himself. Cooler brains than his should devise a fitting means of exposure, and should bring retribution upon the traitor and schemer. This decided, they talked of minor matters affecting the main issue. John Dixon expressed a wish to see Robert Grantham without himself being seen—for even now at odd moments a kind of wondering doubt stole upon him whether all he had heard was true—and Rathbeal, ripe in expedients, suggested the way to this.

"At ten o'clock to-night," he said, "come to the entrance to Charing Cross Station, and I will pass you in the company of Robert Grantham; then you will have an opportunity of seeing him. Do not accost us; but having satisfied yourself, take your departure. I can easily manage to bring Grantham to the spot, and to-morrow I will call upon you at any hour you name."

Upon this understanding they separated, Rathbeal well satisfied with his day's work, and glowing with anticipation of the enemy's overthrow.

"You do wrong to make enemies, shrewd sir" (thus his thoughts ran); "they are more zealous against you, more determined for victory, when they scent the coming battle. You are a fool, shrewd sir, for all your cleverness. Your sun is setting, and you see not the shadows beyond. But the veil shall soon be drawn by willing hands. With what truth could Robert say:

, as thou knowest, went forth, and my heart with sorrow oppressed,
Where ruthless Fate had bestowed what I needed for life and rest.

We are but instruments in the hands of Fate. Sooner or later the ax shall fall."

He had an idle hour before his appointment with Robert Grantham, and instinctively he had turned his steps in the direction of Mr. Fox-Cordery's house. As he walked on the opposite side of the street he saw a miserably-clad woman, whose face, equally with her dress, was a melancholy index to her woeful state, standing at the door, exchanging words with a servant who had responded to her knock. Crossing the road, he heard something of what was passing between them, and learned that Mr. Fox-Cordery was in the country. Closer contact with the woman disclosed more plainly to him that she was destitute and in sore trouble, and he was particularly struck at the half-defiant and wholly reckless tone in which she spoke. The door was shut upon her, and she was left standing in the street. Then he observed that she directed a threatening and despairing look at the house; and, as she was walking slowly away, he went up and asked her if he could be of any assistance to her, and whether she would tell him what she wanted with Mr. Fox-Cordery. It was Martha he accosted, but she would have nothing to say to him. Bidding him sullenly to mind his own business, she quickened her steps to a run and disappeared. He reproached himself afterward for not hastening after her, and tempting her with a bribe; for he felt that the woman had some bitter grievance against Mr. Fox-Cordery, and that she could have been of assistance in bringing him to bay. But he shrugged his shoulders, muttering "What is, is; what will be, will be," and followed in the direction she had taken, without, however, seeing her again.

CHAPTER XIV.

Do you remember Billy's last prayer?

At ten o'clock that night Rathbeal and Robert Grantham were at Charing Cross Station, as he had engaged they should be. He had no difficulty in wooing Grantham to the neighborhood, in which they had taken many a stroll on leisure nights. He had given his friend an unfaithful version of his interview with the lawyers, saying there was a difficulty in obtaining the information he required, and that he was to call upon them again to-morrow.

"There is a small sum of money attaching to the business," he said, "but we must wait for the precise particulars. It is likely you will have to put in an appearance."

"I will do whatever you advise," said Grantham, "but assist in keeping me out of it till the last moment."

Rathbeal promised, and they strolled to and fro, westward to Trafalgar Square, eastward not farther than Buckingham Street, conversing, as was their wont, on the typical signs of life that thronged this limited space. Robert Grantham was always deeply impressed by these signs which, in their contrasts of joy and misery, and of wealth and poverty, furnish pregnant pictures of the extremes of human existence. Grantham was saying something to this effect when he paused before a white-faced, raggedly-dressed child— no other than Little Prue—who had some boxes of matches in her hands, and was saying to a woman who had also paused to observe her:

"Kind lady! Father's dead, and mother's laying ill of a fever, and baby's dying 'cause we ain't 'ad nothink to eat since yesterday!"

The woman gave Little Prue a penny, and the next moment a man stepped to her side and snatched the penny from her hand, the child making no objection.

"A suggestive scene," said Rathbeal. "The brute is the girl's father, I suppose, and she stands there in the gutter by his directions, probably repeating the speech he has drilled into her. Does not such a picture tempt you not to give? Is it not almost a justification for the existence of institutions which contend that beggary is a preventable disease?"

"Not in my eyes," replied Robert Grantham. "I have no sympathy with anti-natural societies, organized for the suppression of benevolent impulse. The endeavor to deaden charitable feeling, and to inculcate into kindly-hearted people that pity must be guided by a kind of mathematical teaching, is a deplorable mistake. Carry such a teaching out to its natural end, and the sweetest influences of our nature would be lost. Seeing what I have seen, I would not give to that poor child, but I would take her away from the brute: and the first thing I would do would be to set her down before a hot, wholesome meal. Poor little waif! See, Rathbeal, the brute is on the watch on the opposite side. Now, if Providence would take him in hand, and deal out to him what he deserves, we might give the child a foretaste of heaven."

Rathbeal, looking to the opposite side of the road, saw John Dixon approaching them, and in order that he should have a clear view of Grantham he took his friend's arm, and proceeded onward a few yards to a spot which was brilliantly lighted up. John Dixon passed them slowly, and exchanged a look of recognition with Rathbeal, which Grantham did not observe.

"It is time to get home," said Rathbeal, who, now that John Dixon was gone, saw no reason to linger.

"A moment, Rathbeal," said Grantham. "I can't get that child out of my head. Is there no way of doing her an act of kindness without the intervention of the brute?"

Little Prue had just finished another appeal in a weak, languid voice, addressed to no one in particular. She appeared to be dazed as the words dropped slowly from her bloodless lips. She could scarcely keep her eyes open; her frail body began to sway.

"She is fainting," said Rathbeal hurriedly; "the child is overpowered by want and fatigue."

The brute on the opposite side saw this also, and he started forward, not impelled by pity, but with the intention of keeping Little Prue's strength in her by means of threats. A judgment fell upon him. It was as if Providence had heard what Robert Grantham said, and had taken him in hand; for as he was crossing the road in haste he got tangled in a conflict of cabs and omnibuses, and was knocked to the ground. Rathbeal darted forward to see what had happened to him, while Grantham, taking Little Prue's hand, said some gentle words to her, which she was too exhausted to understand. A great crowd had assembled on the spot where the brute had fallen, and Rathbeal, returning, whispered to Grantham that he had been run over.

"What are they doing with him?" asked Grantham.

"They are carrying him to Charing Cross Hospital."

"He will be all right there. If we want to inquire after him we can do so to-morrow. Let us look after the child."

She needed looking after; but for Grantham's sustaining arm she would have sunk into the gutter.

"I know the hospital to take her to," said Grantham, "and the medicine she needs."

With Little Prue in his arms, he plunged into a narrow street, accompanied by Rathbeal, and entered a common restaurant, where he ordered a pot of tea, bread and butter, and a chop. The swift motion through the air had done something to revive Little Prue, the tea and food did the rest; and presently she was eating and drinking as only one who was famished could. The men looked on in wondering pity, and did not interrupt her engrossing labors. It was not until nature was satisfied that she thought of her father; a look of terror flashed into her eyes.

"What's the matter, child?" asked Robert Grantham.

"Father'll be the death of me!" she replied.

"Don't be frightened; he will not hurt you."

"Are you sure, sir? You don't know father!"

"I am quite sure; we have seen him."

This satisfied Little Prue, and the look of terror changed to one of gratitude.

"Thank yer kindly, sir," she said. "I think I should 'ave died if I 'adn't 'ad somethink to eat. It's a long time since I had sech a tuck-out. I couldn't eat another mouthful if I tried."

"And now, child, tell us where you live, and whether you have a mother."

"Oh, yes, sir, I've got a mother; and I live in Roxy's Rents."

"I've heard of the place," said Rathbeal; "it's in Lambeth. We will see the little one home."

"Thank yer, sir. I don't think I could find my way without father. Oh!" she cried, looking about distressfully, "where's my matches?"

They had dropped from her hands when she was falling, and the friends had not stopped to pick them up.

"Never mind your matches."

"But father'll wollup me if I don't sell 'em before I go 'ome! I can't go 'ome till I've got a shilling!"

"You shall have the shilling. Here it is. We will take care of it till we get to Roxy's Rents, and you shall give it to your mother. What is your name, child?"

"Prue, sir; Little Prue."

Robert Grantham laid his hand on Rathbeal's arm.

"Little Prue!" he said. "That is poor Billy's sweetheart, that he spoke of with his dying breath."

He addressed the child:

"Did you know a poor boy called Billy?"

"Oh, yes, sir; we used to play together. He sed he'd marry me when he grew up, if he could get a suit of clothes. What's become of Billy, sir? I ain't seen 'im for a long time."

"He is happier than he was, my child," said Grantham; "all his troubles are over."

"I'm glad to 'ear that, sir. I wish mine and mother's was."

"They will be, one day. Now, child, we must be moving."

Little Prue rose and put her hand in Grantham's and they left the restaurant. They rode to Lambeth by 'bus and tram, and then, being in streets familiar to her, Little Prue conducted them to Roxy's Rents. Her mother's room was in darkness.

"Are yer coming in, sir?"

"Yes; we will see your mother before we leave you."

"Mother, mother!" cried Prue, opening the door.

Mrs. Flower started up and, running to the door, caught her child in her arms.

"O Prue, Prue! where have you been? I was afraid you were lost!"

"I should 'ave been, mother, if it 'adn't been for the gentlemen."

"The gentlemen?"

She could not see them.

"Do not be alarmed," said Robert Grantham. "Your little one was not well, and we brought her home. She is all right now."

"You're very good, sir; I'm ever so much obliged to you."

"Oh, mother, I've 'ad sech a supper! Did yer get the money for the washing?"

She was accustomed to take her part in these domestic matters, which were, in a sense, vital.

"Don't worry, child, before the gentlemen."

"But did yer, mother?" persisted Little Prue, thinking of the chances of food for to-morrow.

"No. There, child, let me alone."

"Have you a candle in the place?" asked Grantham, suspecting the state of affairs.

"No, sir. I am really ashamed—"

"We owe your little one a shilling for some matches," said Grantham, pitying her confusion, and slipping the money into her hand. "Is it too late to buy some candles?"

He would have taken his departure under these awkward circumstances, but he considered it his duty to tell Mrs. Flower of the accident that had happened to her husband.

"One of the lodgers will sell me one, sir, if you don't mind waiting."

"We will wait."

"Martha!" called Mrs. Flower; but Martha was asleep, and did not speak. "It's my sister, sir; I thought she might be awake. I won't be gone a minute."

She ran to another room, and obtaining the candle, returned with it alight. Her visitors sighed at the misery it displayed. Martha's arms were spread upon the table, and her head rested upon them. Prue pulled her mother's dress.

"Who is she, mother?"

"Your aunt Martha."

Prue went to the sleeping woman, and tried to get a glimpse of her face.

"I have bad news to tell you about your husband," said Grantham, speaking low, so that the child should not hear. "He has met with an accident, and has been taken to Charing Cross Hospital."

He broke the news to her in a gentle voice, and she received it without emotion. Her husband had crushed all love for him from her breast long since, and she had felt for years that it would be a happy release if he were dead.

"Is he much hurt, sir?" she asked, with tearless eyes.

"I do not know. He was knocked down by a cab, and was carried to the hospital at once. He will be better cared for there than here."

"Yes, sir; I have no money to pay for doctors. Did Prue see the accident?"

"She knows nothing of it."

"Drip—drip—drip! Oh, God! will it never stop?"

It was Martha who was speaking. The men were awed by the despairing voice.

"It's my sister, sir; I told you, I think. She came upon me quite sudden to-night. I haven't seen her for years. She's in trouble. Martha, Martha!"

She shook the woman, who started wildly to her feet and looked this way and that with swift glances, more like a hunted animal than a human creature.

Rathbeal uttered an exclamation. It was the woman he had seen that afternoon standing at Mr. Fox-Cordery's door.

"Fate!" he said, and advanced toward her.

A violent spasm of fear seized Martha, and shook her in every limb. Crazed perhaps by her dreams, or terrified by the suspicion of a hidden evil in the appearance of Rathbeal, whom she instantly recognized, and who must have tracked her down for some new oppression, she retreated as he advanced, and watching her opportunity, rushed past him from the room, and flew into the dark shelter of the streets. They gazed after her in astonishment, and then followed her into the alley, and thence into the wider thoroughfare, but they saw no trace of her.

"Her troubles have driven her mad," said Mrs. Flower, "and no wonder.

How she's lived through them is a mystery. She's in such a state that I'm afraid she'll do herself a mischief."

"I intended her no harm," said Rathbeal. "I saw her once before to-day, and if my suspicions are well founded, it may be in my power to render her a service, even to obtain some kind of justice for her, if her troubles are caused by a man."

"A man, you call him!" said Mrs. Flower, with bitter emphasis.

"Do you know him?"

"I heard his name for the first time to-night."

"Is it Fox-Cordery?"

In the dark he felt Robert Grantham give a start, and he pressed his arm as a warning to be silent.

"That's the villain that's brought her to this; that took her away from her home and disgraced her, and then left her to starve. If there's justice in heaven, he ought to be made suffer for it."

"There's justice in heaven," said Rathbeal, "and it shall overtake him. Your sister needs a man to champion her cause; I offer myself as that man. Without a powerful defender, the reptile who has brought this misery upon her will spurn and laugh at her. It is too late to talk together to-night; your child is waiting for you, and your sister may return at any moment. After a night's rest, she will listen to me—will believe in me. May I call upon you to-morrow morning early?"

"Yes, sir, as early as you like. I get up at six. You speak fair, and you've been kind to Prue. God bless you for your goodness! I shall have to go to the hospital in the morning, but I'll wait at home till ten for you."

"Very well. Meanwhile, this may be of service to you."

He gave her two shillings, and wishing her goodnight, the friends took their departure.

"What does all this mean, Rathbeal?" asked Robert Grantham. "I am wrapt in mystery."

"You trust me, Robert?"

"I would trust you with my life."

"Then believe that I have my reasons for keeping silence to-night. Before long the mystery shall be explained to you. I am working for your happiness, Robert."

"For my happiness?" echoed Grantham, with a groan.

"You are not a skeptic? You believe in eternal mercy and justice?"

"I do, God help me!"

"Hold fast to that belief. The clouds are breaking, and I see a light shining on your life. Do you remember poor Billy's last prayer?' O Lord God, give Mr. Gran all he wants, and a bit over!' The Lord of the Universe heard that prayer. Ask me no questions, but before you go to bed to-night pray with a thankful heart; for the age of miracles is not yet over, Robert, my friend."

CHAPTER XV.

Friends in Council.

Rathbeal presented himself at Mrs. Flower's room as the clock struck nine. In anticipation of his visit, the woman had "tidied" up the apartment, and Little Prue looked quite neat, with her hands and face washed, and her hair properly combed and brushed. Rathbeal's two shillings had enabled them to have a sufficient breakfast, and the child, naturally shy, raised her eyes gratefully to her benefactor.

"Well, little one," he said, pinching her cheek, "do you feel better this morning?"

"Oh, ever so much, sir!" replied Little Prue.

He looked round for Martha, and Mrs. Flower told him sorrowfully that her sister had not come back.

"I shall be worried out of my life till I see her, sir," she said.

"We will try and find her for you," he said. "And now tell me everything you know concerning her."

She related all that she had learned from Martha; and when she had done he plied her with questions, which she answered freely. Having obtained all the information it was in her power to give him, and leaving his address with her, he rode to Craven Street, his appointment with John Dixon having been made for an early hour. He was received with cordiality all John Dixon's suspicions being now quite dispelled.

"I recognized Robert Grantham the moment I saw him," he said, "thanks to his wearing no hair on his face; but it bears the marks of deep suffering."

"He has passed through the fire," said Rathbeal. "I have more news for you. Another weapon against Mr. Fox-Cordery is placed in our hands."

With that he gave an account of his adventures with Martha and Little Prue, to which John Dixon listened with grave attention, and then said he had also news to impart.

"It will be necessary, I think," he said, "to strike earlier than we expected. You will be surprised to hear that I expect shortly to be connected with Mr. Fox-Cordery by marriage. I have no wish to spare him on that account, but for the sake of my intended wife I should wish, if possible, to avoid a public exposure. Justice must be done to Robert Grantham and his wife and child— that is imperative; and if we can compel Mr. Fox-Cordery privately to make some reparation to the poor woman who has so strangely been introduced into this bad business, so much the better. It is likely, however, that she will disappear from the scene; my opinion is that she will not return to her sister. So far as she is concerned, there is no law to touch her betrayer: her case, unhappily, is a common one, and he can snap his fingers at her; and, moreover, if she personally annoy him, he can prosecute her. But he may be willing to sacrifice something to prevent his name being dragged into the papers. As for any punishment he may have incurred for his infamous conduct toward the Granthams, the choice of visiting it upon him must be left to your friend. Speaking as a lawyer, we have no standing in the matter: it is not us he has wronged; we are simple lookers on."

"May I ask how you expect to be connected with Mr. Fox-Cordery by marriage?"

"There is now no secret about it. He has a sister, whom he has oppressed after his own brutal fashion since she was a child. That two natures so opposite as theirs should be born of the same parents is a mystery beyond my comprehension, but so it is. She is the personification of sweetness and charity, but I will not dilate upon her virtues. It is enough that I am engaged to be married to her, and that the engagement is viewed with intense dislike by her brother and her mother, both of whom would, I have not the least doubt, he rejoiced to hear that I had met my death in a railway accident or by some equally agreeable means. It is, I believe, chiefly because of her liking for my intended wife that Mrs. Grantham accepted the invitation of Mr. Fox-Cordery to become a guest in the house by the river which he has taken for the summer months. Besides, you must bear in mind that he is Mrs. Grantham's business agent, and that she is ignorant of his true character. I have an idea that her eyes are being opened, for I have received a letter from my intended this morning in which she informs me that Mrs. Grantham is in great trouble, and wishes to consult me privately. She asks me to meet her to-night near her brother's house, when I shall hear what the trouble is. I am prepared for some fresh villainy on the part of Mr. Fox-Cordery, who has entertained a passion for Mrs. Grantham for years. He knew her in her maiden days, and would have paid open suit to her, but her love was given to Robert Grantham."

"Do you tell me that he desires to marry her now?"

"I understand from Charlotte—the name of my intended; I cannot speak of her as Miss Fox-Cordery, there is something hateful in the name—that it is his ardent wish, and that he has set his heart upon it. That may be the reason for his taking the house by the river and for his wish to make Mrs. Grantham his guest there. Part of a plan—and his plans are generally well laid. He hoped to bring his suit to a happy ending, for him, before the termination of her visit."

"But Robert Grantham lives!" exclaimed Rathbeal.

"He believes him to be dead, remember; you yourself told me so."

"Yes, yes; I was forgetting for the moment. I see now why he came to me; the motive of all his actions is clear. But this must not be allowed to go on any longer. In justice to her, in justice to Robert, the truth must no longer be withheld."

"My own opinion: there has been but little time lost; it is only yesterday that you and I first met. My idea is, to bring matters to a conclusion this very night. I shall go to meet my intended, and hear what she has to say. I am not sure whether Mrs. Grantham will be with her. If she is not, I will not leave without an interview in which she shall learn the solemn truth. It will be a difficult task to prepare her for it, but it is a duty that must be performed. Meanwhile you must prepare Robert Grantham for the wonderful happiness in store for him. Do you think it advisable that we shall go down together?"

"It will be best; and on our way we can determine upon our course of action. I imagine that we shall have to keep in the background until we receive an intimation from you to appear; but we can talk of all that by-and-by. I have paved the way with Robert already, and he is now impatiently awaiting me. Ah-ha! Mr. Fox-Cordery, when you weave a web, nothing ever escapes from it! A stronger hand than yours has woven for you a web, and scattered yours to the four winds of heaven. I have tortured him already with letters, trusting to Fate to aid me, and he stands, unmasked, defeated, disgraced for evermore."

This outburst was enigmatical to John Dixon, but time was too valuable for him to ask for an explanation. There was much to do, and every minute of the day would be occupied. He made an appointment to meet Rathbeal and Grantham in the evening, and they parted to go upon their separate tasks.

CHAPTER XVI

Mr. Fox-Cordery's Master-Stroke.

Mr. Fox-Cordery had made the move he had thought of to insure success. On the morning of the day that Charlotte wrote to John Dixon to come to her, he sent word to Mrs. Grantham that he wished to see her upon business of importance, either in his room or hers. She sent word back that she would see him in her apartment, and he went there to deal a master-stroke. Her child Clair was with her, and Charlotte also; and he drew Clair to him, and spent a few moments in endearments which manifestly did not give the girl any pleasure. He had not succeeded in making himself a favorite with her, and as soon as she could she escaped from him and ran to her mother's side. He was quite aware that Clair was not fond of him, but he made no protest; the future should pay him for all. Mrs. Grantham and Charlotte were both employed in needlework, and they did not lay it aside when he entered.

"Charlotte!" he said, sternly.

"Yes, Fox," she answered.

He motioned with his head to the door, indicating that she was to leave the room. Charlotte rose immediately.

"Where are you going, Charlotte?" asked Mrs. Grantham.

He replied for her.

"I wish to speak to you alone," he said. "Take Clair with you, Charlotte, and go and gather some flowers."

"You can speak before them," said Mrs. Grantham; "they will be very quiet."

"Yes, mamma," said Clair, "we will be very quiet."

"What I have to say is for your ears alone," he said, and he motioned again to the door. The masterfulness of the order did not escape Mrs. Grantham. She moved her chair to the window, which looked out upon the lawn, and from which she could also see the bridge.

"Go with Charlotte, my dear," she said to Clair, "but keep on the lawn, so that I can see you."

"Yes, mamma."

"My dear Mrs. Grantham," commenced Mr. Fox-Cordery, in a bland voice of false pity, "I have deplorable news to convey to you. A short time since, when I had the honor of making a proposal to you—"

The look she gave him stopped him. "If you are about to renew that proposal, Mr. Fox-Cordery, I must ask you to go no further. I gave you my answer then; it would be my answer now."

"I am unfortunate in my choice of words," he said, losing the guard he had kept upon himself during her visit. "I did not wish to shock you too suddenly by disclosing abruptly what it is my duty, as your man of business, to disclose."

"To shock me too suddenly!" she said, pausing in her work.

"It was my desire. Believe me, I am your friend, as I have ever been; make any call you like upon me, and you will not find me unwilling to respond. But to come down so low in the world, to lose one's all, to be suddenly beggared—"

He put his hand to his eyes, and watched slyly through his fingers. Her work dropped into her lap; her mouth trembled, but she did not speak.

"It might have been borne with resignation," he continued, "if one did not have a beloved child to care for and protect from the hardships of a cruel world. In your place I can imagine how it would affect me, how I should tremble at what is before me. Love is all-powerful, but there are circumstances in which it brings inexpressible grief to the heart. How shall I tell you? I cannot, I cannot!"

He rose from his chair, and paced the room with downcast head, but he kept his stealthy watch upon her face all the time. He was disconcerted that she did not speak, that she uttered no cry of alarm. He expected her to assist him through the scene he had acted to himself a dozen times. He had put words into her mouth, natural words which should by rights have been spoken in the broken periods of his revelation; but she sat quite silent, waiting for him to proceed.

"Still, it must be told, and should have been told before. I grieve to say that you have lost your fortune, and that, unless you have resources with which I am unacquainted—and with all my heart I hope you have—your future and the future of your dear child is totally unprovided for."

And having come to this termination, he threw himself into his chair with the air of a man whose own hopes and prospects were utterly blighted. She found her voice.

"How have I lost my fortune, sir?" she asked with dry lips. Her throat was parched, and her husky voice had a note of pain in it which satisfied him that he had succeeded in terrifying her. "You had the sole control of it."

"Alas, yes! How ardently do I wish that it had been in the control of another man, to whom you were indifferent, and who could have told you calmly what it shakes me to the soul to tell! I have also lost, but I can afford it; it is only a portion of my fortune that has gone down in wreck. I have still a competence left that makes me independent of the buffets of the world, that enables me to provide a home for those I love."

"I fail to understand you, sir," she said, glancing from the window at her child, who was walking on the lawn with Charlotte, and who, seeing her mother looking at her, smiled and kissed her hand to her. "You have not yet informed me how I have lost my fortune."

"You made investments—"

"Acting upon your advice, sir."

"True; I believed my advice to be good, and I invested part of my money also in the same stocks and shares. Unhappily the papers you have signed—"

"Always by your directions, sir. You informed me that the investments were good, and that I need have no anxiety."

"I cannot deny it; I was wrong, foolishly, madly wrong. I thought your fortune would be doubled, trebled. It has turned out disastrously, every shilling you possessed is lost. And, unhappily, as I was saying, the papers you have signed have involved you beyond the extent of your means. It racks me to think of what is before you, unless you accept the assistance which a friend is ready to tender you. A life of poverty, of privation for you and your dear child—it maddens me to think of it!"

"For how long have you known this?" she asked faintly.

It was the question he wished her to put to him.

"I knew it," he said humbly, "when I made the proposal which you rejected. I knew then that you were ruined, and it was my desire to spare you.

131

Had you answered as my heart led me to hope you would have done, I still should have kept the secret from your knowledge until the day that made you mine, to love, to shelter, to protect. It is the truth, dear Mrs. Grantham—it is the truth, on the word of an honorable gentleman."

He put his hand to his heart, and sighed heavily.

"I cannot but believe you," said Mrs. Grantham, pondering more upon his manner than the words he uttered; it seemed to her as if a light had suddenly descended upon her, through which she saw for the first time the true character of the man she had trusted. "I cannot but believe you when you tell me I am ruined, and that starvation lies before me and my child."

"Alas!" he put in here. "Your child, your dear Clair!"

"I had no understanding of business, and I relied implicitly upon you. I never questioned, never for a moment doubted."

"Nor I," he murmured. "Am I not a sufferer, like yourself? Does that not prove how confident I was that I was acting for the best? Call me foolish, headstrong, if you will; inflict any penance you please upon me, and I am by your side to bear it."

She shivered inwardly at the insidious tenderness he threw into his voice, but she was at the same time careful to conceal this feeling. She was in his power; her whole future was in his hands, and with it the future of her beloved Clair. She had no other friend; she could not think of another being in the world whom she could ask for help at this critical juncture. It seemed as if the very bread she and her child ate from this day forth might depend upon him who had brought ruin upon them.

"Yes," he continued, "I will not desert you. A single word from your lips, and your misfortune will become a blessing."

"Is nothing left, sir?" she asked. "Have I really lost everything?"

"You are cruel to make me repeat what I have said, what I have endeavored to make clear to you. You have not only lost everything, but are responsible for obligations it is, I am afraid, out of your power to discharge. Mrs. Grantham, will you listen to me?"

"I have listened patiently, sir. Have you any other misfortunes to make clear to me?"

"None, I am thankful to say. You know all; there is nothing to add to the sad news I have been compelled to impart. Think only of yourself and your dear child."

"I am thinking of her, sir."

"She is not strong; she has not been accustomed to endure poverty. Can we not save her from its stings? Is it not a duty?"

"To me, sir, a sacred duty, if I can see a way."

"Let me show you the way," he said eagerly. "Dear Mrs. Grantham, my feelings are unchanged. Even in your maiden days I loved you, but stifled my love and kept it buried in my breast when I saw that another had taken the place it was the wish of my heart to occupy. You gave to another the love for which I yearned, and I looked on and suffered in silence. Is not my devotion worthy of a reward? It is in your power to bestow it; it is in your power to save dear Clair from a life of misery. I renew the offer I made you. Promise to become my wife, and the grievous loss you have sustained need not give you a moment's anxiety."

The artificial modulation of his tones, his elaborate actions, and his evident desire to impress her with a sense of the nobility of his offer, filled her with a kind of loathing for him. It was as though he held out an iron chain, and warned her that if she refused to be bound she was condemning her child to poverty and despair. But agonizing as was this reflection, she could not speak the words he wished to hear; she felt that she _must_ have time to think.

"What you have told me," she said, "is so unexpected, I was so little prepared for it, that it would not be fair to answer you immediately. My mind is confused; pray do not press me; in a little while I shall be calmer, and then—"

"And then," he said, taking up her words and thinking the battle won, "you will see that it is the only road of happiness left open to you, and you will give me a favorable answer. We will tread this road together, and enjoy life's pleasures. Shall we say this evening?" She shook her head. "To-morrow, then?"

"Give me another day," she pleaded.

"Till the day after to-morrow, by all means," he said gayly. "It would be ungallant to refuse. But, dear Mrs. Grantham—may I not rather say dear Lucy?—it must be positively the day after to-morrow. I shall count the minutes. To be long in your society in a state of suspense, or in the knowledge that you refuse to be mine, would be more than I can bear."

She silently construed these words; they conveyed a threat. If in two days she did not give him a favorable answer, she and Clair would have to leave the house at once, and go forth into the world, stripped and beggared.

"And now I will leave you," he said, taking her hand and kissing it. "Do not look at the cloud, dear Lucy—look only at the silver lining."

He was about to go, when she said:

"Mr. Fox-Cordery, if I wish to speak to a friend, can I do so here, in your house?"

"Why, surely here," he replied, wondering who the friend could be, and feeling it would be best for him that the meeting should be an open and not a secret one. "Where else but in the home in which you are mistress?"

She thanked him, and he kissed her hand again, and looked languishingly at her lips, and then left her to her reflections.

She locked her door, and devoted herself to a consideration of her despairing position. She tried in vain to recollect what papers she had signed; there had been many from time to time, and she had had such confidence in the man who had managed her husband's affairs, and since his death had managed hers, that when he said, "Put your name here, where my finger is, Mrs. Grantham," she had grown into the habit of obeying without reading what she signed. The longer she thought, the more she grew confused. There was but little time for decision, scarcely two days. Where could she turn for counsel? Where could she find a friend who might be able to point out a way of escape? She stood at the window as she asked these questions of herself, and as her eyes wandered over the prospect they lighted upon Charlotte. The moment they did so she thought of John Dixon. The questions were answered. She would implore Charlotte to bring about an interview with him.

Under ordinary circumstances she would not have dreamt of asking a sister of Mr. Fox-Cordery to assist her in opposing his wishes, but the circumstances were not ordinary. These last few days Mr. Fox-Cordery and his mother had thrown off the mask in their treatment of Charlotte, and Mrs. Grantham had noticed with pain the complete want of affection they displayed. She had spoken sympathetically to Charlotte of this altered behavior, and Charlotte had answered wearily that she had been accustomed to it all her life. The pitiful confession made Mrs. Grantham very tender toward her, and she consoled Charlotte with much feeling. Then Charlotte poured forth her full heart, and it needed but little persuasion to cause her to relate the story of her lifelong oppression. The bond of affection which united the women was drawn still closer, and they exchanged confidences without reserve. Now, in her own hour of trouble, Mrs. Grantham sought Charlotte, and confided to her the full extent of the misfortune that had overtaken her.

"If I could see your John," she said, "he might be able to advise me perhaps."

"I will write to him," said Charlotte impulsively; "he will come at once."

And so it was arranged. A little later, Mrs. Grantham said:

"I must not anger your brother by meeting John secretly. You shall meet him, and ask him to come and speak to me here in my own room."

"But may he?" inquired Charlotte.

"Your brother has given me permission to receive in this house any friend I wish to consult. There is no one else in the world whose advice I can rely upon; I am sure your John is a true and sincere gentleman. Will it make any difference to you, Charlotte, if your brother discovers that you have assisted to bring about this meeting?"

"None," replied Charlotte, in a decided tone. "I ought to know him by this time. He made me a half-promise that he would give me a little money to buy a few clothes, but the way he has behaved to me lately proves that he has no intention of helping me. I shall have to go to John as I am."

Then the women spent an hour in mutual consolation, and exchanged vows that nothing should ever weaken their affection for each other.

"John will be your true friend," said Charlotte, "remember that. You may believe every word he says. Oh, my dear, I hope things will turn out better than they look!"

"I put my trust in God," said Mrs. Grantham solemnly, and, clasping her hands, raised her eyes in silent prayer.

CHAPTER XVII.

Retribution.

At five o'clock in the evening Robert Grantham and Rathbeal joined John Dixon in his rooms in Craven Street. The revelation which Rathbeal had made to Grantham had produced a marked change in him. With wonder and incredulity had he listened at first to the strange story, but his friend's impressive earnestness had gradually convinced him that it was no fable which Rathbeal was relating. The first force of his emotions spent, hope, humility, and thankfulness were expressed in his face. It seemed to him that the meeting between him and his wife, which Rathbeal had promised should take place that night, was like the meeting of two spirits that had been wandering for ages in darkness. It was not without fear that he looked forward to it. The sense of the wrong he had inflicted upon the woman he had vowed to cherish and protect was as strong within him now as it had been through all these years, from the day upon which he heard that she was dead. Would she accept his assurance that he had not been false to her, would she believe in his repentance, would she forgive him?

"I ask but that," he said to Rathbeal, "and then I shall be content to go my way, and spend the rest of my life in the task of self-purification."

"Hope for something better," Rathbeal replied: "for a reunion of hearts, for a good woman's full forgiveness, and forgetfulness of the errors of the past. The clouds have not lifted only to deceive. There is a bright future before you, my friend."

"My future is in God's hands," said Grantham.

"He will direct your wife aright. Hope and believe."

In this spirit they wended their way to John Dixon's rooms.

Grantham and he had not met since they left school, but he received his old schoolfellow as though there had been no break in their early association. They shook hands warmly, and the look that passed between Rathbeal and John Dixon told the latter that the truth had been revealed to the wronged man. They wasted no time in idle conversation, but started immediately on their journey.

For a reason which he did not divulge to his companions, John Dixon had elected to drive to Mr. Fox-Cordery's summer residence; he had a vague idea that occasion might arise to render it necessary that he should run off with Charlotte that very night; if so, there was a carriage, with a pair of smart horses, at his command. The coachman he had engaged had received his instructions, and when they got out of the tangle of the crowded thoroughfares the horses galloped freely along the road. While they proceed upon their way some information must be given of Martha's movements.

She had rushed from her sister's room in a state of delirium. Her privations and sufferings, and the conflicting emotions which tortured her, had destroyed her mental balance, and she was not responsible for her actions. She had no settled notion where she was going; the only motive by which she was guided was her desire to escape from her fellow-creatures. Instinctively she chose the least frequented roads, and she stumbled blindly on till she was out of London streets. She had no food, and no money to purchase it, but she scarcely felt her hunger. One dominant idea possessed her—under the floating clouds and with silence all around her, she heard the drip of water. It pierced the air, it made itself felt as well as heard. Drip, drip, drip! The sound wooed her on toward the valley of the Thames, and unconsciously she pursued a route which had been familiar to her in her girlhood's days. She walked all that night, and through the whole of the following day, compelled to stop now and again for rest, but doing so always when there was a danger of her being accosted by persons who approached her from an opposite direction. Rathbeal, had he been acquainted with her movements, would have answered the question whether it was chance or fate that took her in the direction of Mr. Fox-Cordery's house. When night came on again she was wandering along the banks of the Thames, within a short distance of the man who had wrecked her life. She knew that she had reached her haven, and she only waited for the moment to put her desperate resolve into execution. The water looked so peaceful and shining! The tide silently lapped the shore, but she heard the drip, drip, drip of the water. Death held out its arms to her, and invited her to its embrace. It was a starlight night, but she saw no stars in heaven. The moon sailed on, but she saw no light. "I shall soon be at rest." That was her thought, if it can be said that she thought at all.

The occupants of a carriage, drawn by a pair of smart horses, saw the figure of a woman moving slowly on toward the little rustic bridge which stretched from Mr. Fox-Cordery's lawn to the opposite bank. They took no notice of her, being entirely occupied with the important mission upon which they were engaged. They had remarked that it was fortunate the night was so fine. Could they have heard the sound that sounded like a death-knell in Martha's ears, they might have changed their minds, and recognized that no night could be fine which bore so despairing a message to a mortal's ears. Drip, drip, drip! "I am coming," whispered Martha to her soul. "I am coming. The water is deep beneath that bridge!"

At nine o'clock Robert Grantham and his companions reached their destination. The coachman drew up at an inn, and the men alighted.

"Now," said John Dixon, as they strolled toward Mr. Fox-Cordery's house, "we must be guided by Charlotte's instructions. The night is so clear that we shall be able to see each other from a distance. You must not be in sight when Charlotte comes; I must explain matters to her. The bank by that bridge stands high. Go there and remain till you hear from me. Before I enter the house I shall have a word to say as to the method of our proceedings. Someone is coming toward us. Yes, it is Charlotte. Go at once, and keep wide of her."

They obeyed, and walked toward the bridge. Martha was on the opposite side, and perceiving men approaching, she crouched down and waited.

"John," said Charlotte, in a low, clear voice.

"Charlotte!"

Only a moment for a loving embrace, and then they began to converse. What they said to each other did not occupy many minutes. John Dixon left her standing alone, and went to his friends.

"I am going to the house," he said, "and am to speak to Mrs. Grantham"—how Robert trembled at the utterance of the name!—"in her room. That is her window; there is a light in the room. If I come to the window and wave a white handkerchief, follow me into the house without question. Allow no one to stop you. I do not know how long I may be there, but I will bring matters to an issue as soon as possible."

They nodded compliance, and Robert Grantham breathed a prayer. Then John Dixon rejoined Charlotte, and they entered the house.

Martha, crouching by the bridge, heard nothing of this. All she heard was the drip of water; all she saw were the dark shadows of men on the opposite side. They would soon be gone, and then, and then—

Mr. Fox-Cordery and his mother, being closeted together, were not aware of the entrance of John Dixon. Unobstructed he ascended the stairs to the first floor, and was conducted to the presence of Mrs. Grantham.

What she had to disclose to him, and what he had to disclose to her, is already known to the reader. She told her story first, and John Dixon said that, from his knowledge of Mr. Fox-Cordery, he was more than inclined to believe that her agent had been false to his trust. He informed her that he had gained an insight into her affairs during the time he had served Mr. Fox-Cordery, and that their disagreement had arisen partly from a remonstrance he had made as to his employer's management of certain speculations.

"My impression was then," said John Dixon, "that Mr. Fox-Cordery was exceeding his powers, and that in case of a loss he could be made responsible for it."

"God bless you for those words!" exclaimed Mrs. Grantham. "The thought of being forced into marriage with him makes me shudder. But what can I do? To see my child in want of food would break my heart."

"There is no question of a marriage with him," said John Dixon gravely; his own task was approaching. "It is impossible. I will tell you why presently, Mrs. Grantham. You will need all your strength. It is not on your affairs alone that I am here to-night. Before I say what I am come to say, let us finish with Mr. Fox-Cordery. I am a partner in a respectable firm of solicitors, and my advice is that you place your business affairs in our hands. We shall demand papers, and a strict investigation; and I think I can promise you that we shall be able to save something substantial for you. Are you agreeable to this course?"

"Yes, dear friend, yes."

"Then I understand from this moment I am empowered to act for you?"

"It is so," she replied, and thanked Heaven for having sent her this friend and comforter.

"Thank Charlotte also," he said.

Then he began to speak of the important branch of his visit to her. Delicately and gently he led up to it; with the tenderness of a true and tender-hearted man he brought the solemn truth before her. With dilating eyes and throbbing breast she listened to the wonderful revelation, and to the description of the life her husband had led since he had received the false news of her death. Much of this he had learned from Rathbeal, who had armed him with the truth; and as he went on the scales fell from her eyes, and she saw with the eyes of her heart the man she had loved, weak, erring, and misguided, but now truly repentant and reformed, and not the guilty being she had been led by Mr. Fox-Cordery to believe he was. She had no thought for the wretch who had worked out his infamous design; she thought only that Robert was true to her, and that her dear child was not fatherless. John Dixon gave her time for this to sink into her mind, and then told her that her husband had accompanied him, and was waiting outside for the signal of joy.

"I will go to him! I will go to him!" she cried.

But John Dixon restrained her.

"Let him come into the house," he said. "Let your enemy know that he is here, and that his schemes are foiled. Remember, I am your adviser. Be guided by me.'"

Trembling in every limb, she went to the window and opened it.

"Shall I give him the signal?" asked John Dixon.

"No; I will do it," she replied, and, reaching forth, waved the white flag of love and forgiveness.

Robert Grantham, his eyes fixed in painful anxiety upon the window, was the first to see the signal. With a gasp of joy he started for the house, and Rathbeal, whose attention just then had been diverted by the figure of Martha crouching by the bridge, hearing his footsteps, turned to follow him. At the moment of his doing so, Martha, seeing them walk away, crept on to the bridge and leaned over. Suddenly she straightened herself, and raising her arms aloft, whispered softly, "I'm coming—I'm coming!" and let herself fall into the water. The heavy splash, accompanied by a muffled scream, reached Rathbeal's ears before he had proceeded twenty yards. Turning to the bridge, and missing the figure of the crouching woman, he instinctively divined what had happened.

"Don't stop for me," he cried hurriedly to Grantham. "I'll follow you."

Then he ran back to the bridge.

Robert Grantham did not hear him, so absorbed was he in the supreme moment that was approaching. Had a storm burst upon him, he would scarcely have been conscious of it. Who was that standing at the window, waving the handkerchief! It was not John Dixon. His eyes were dim, his heart palpitated violently, as he fancied he recognized the form of his wife. If it were so, indeed his hope was answered. He was met at the door by Charlotte, who led him to the room above. Standing upon the threshold he saw his wife looking with wistful yearning toward him—toward her husband who, after these long years, had come to her, as it were, from the grave. They were spellbound for a few moments, incapable of speech or motion, each gazing upon the other for a sign.

John Dixon stepped noiselessly to Charlotte's side, and the lovers left the room hand in hand, closing the door gently behind them.

Husband and wife, so strangely reunited, were alone.

She was the first to move. Bending forward, she held out her arms, and her eyes shone with ineffable love; with a sob he advanced, and fell upon his knees before her. Sinking into a chair, she drew his head to her breast and folded her arms around him.

Let the veil fall upon those sacred minutes. Aching hearts were eased, faith was restored, and Love shed its holy light upon Lucy and Robert.

"Our child!" he whispered. "Our Clair!"

"I will take you to her," she said, and led him to the bed where Clair was sleeping.

Meanwhile Rathbeal, hastening to the bridge, saw his suspicions confirmed by the death-bubbles rising to the surface of the water. With the energy and rapidity of a young man, he tore off his coat and waistcoat, and plunged into the river. He was a grand swimmer, and he did not lose his self-possession. He had eyes in his hands and fingers, and when, after some time had elapsed, he grasped a woman's hair, he struck out for the bank, and reaching it in safety, drew the woman after him. She lay inanimate upon the bank, and, clearing his eyes of the water, he knelt down to ascertain if he had rescued her in time to save her. He put his ear to her heart, his mouth to her mouth, but she gave no sign of life. The moon, which had been hidden behind a cloud, now sailed forth into the clearer space of heaven, and its beams illumined the woman's face.

"It is Martha!" he cried, and without a moment's hesitation he caught her up in his arms and ran with her to the house.

Mr. Fox-Cordery, closeted with his mother in a room on the ground floor, heard sounds upon the stairs which had a disturbing effect upon him. The sounds were those of strange footsteps and whispering voices. Opening the door quickly he saw, by the light of the hall-lamp, John Dixon and Charlotte coming down—John with his arm round Charlotte's waist, she inclining tenderly toward the man she loved.

"You here!" cried Mr. Fox-Cordery.

"You behold no spirit," replied John Dixon, releasing Charlotte, and placing her behind him; "I am honest flesh and blood."

Mr. Fox-Cordery, his mother now by his side, looked from John Dixon to Charlotte with a spiteful venom in his eyes which found vent in his voice.

"You drab!" he cried. "You low-minded hussy! And you, you sneak and rogue! Have you conspired to rob the house? I'll have the law of you; you shall stand in the dock together. Curse the pair of you!"

"Easy, easy," said John Dixon, calm and composed. "Don't talk so freely of law and docks. And don't forget that curses come home to roost."

Other sounds from the first floor distracted Mr. Fox-Cordery.

"Is there a gang of you here? Whose steps are those above? Mother, alarm the house. Call up the servants, and send for the police."

"Aye, do," said John Dixon, as Mrs. Fox-Cordery pulled the bell with violence, "and let them see and hear what you shall see and hear. Don't be frightened, Charlotte. The truth must out now."

Mr. Fox-Cordery's pallid lips quivered, and he started back with a smothered shriek. Robert Grantham and his wife appeared at the top of the stairs, and as they slowly descended he retreated step by step, and seized his mother's arm.

"Be quiet, can't you?" he hissed. "Go and send the servants away. We do not want them. Say it was a mistake—a false alarm—anything—but keep them in their rooms!"

Retribution stared him in the face. The edifice he had built up with so much care had toppled over, and he was entangled in the ruins. It was well for them that he had no weapon in his hands, for coward as he was, his frenzy would have impelled him to use it upon them.

"I am here," said John Dixon, "by the permission you gave to Mrs. Grantham, and I am armed with authority to act for her. You see, I have not come alone."

"You devil! you devil!" muttered Mr. Fox-Cordery, through the foam that gathered about his mouth.

"Say nothing more to him, Mr. Dixon," said Robert Grantham, who had reached the foot of the stairs. "The truth has been brought to light, and his unutterable villainy is fully exposed. Leave to the future what is yet to be done. Lucy, go and dress our child. We quit this house within the hour. Do not fear; no one shall follow you."

Mrs. Grantham went upstairs to Clair, and she had scarcely reached the room when the street door was burst open, and Rathbeal appeared with Martha in his arms.

"This poor woman threw herself into the water," said Rathbeal. "Tired of life, she sought the peace of death in the river. Give way, Mr. Fox-Cordery; she must be attended to without delay. Obstruct us, and the crime of murder will be on your soul!" He beat Mr. Fox-Cordery back into the room, and laid his burden down on the floor. "You see who it is!"

"She is a stranger to me," muttered Mr. Fox-Cordery, his heart quaking with fear.

"False! You know her well. If she is dead you will be made responsible; for you and no other drove her to her death!"

It was no time to bandy further words. Assisted by Charlotte and John Dixon, he set to work in the task of bringing respiration into the inanimate form, Mr. Fox-Cordery and his mother standing silently by, while Robert Grantham guarded the staircase. Their efforts were successful. In a quarter of an hour Martha gave faint signs of life, and they redoubled their efforts. Martha opened her eyes, and they fell upon Mr. Fox-Cordery.

"That man! that monster!" she murmured, and would have risen, but her strength failed her.

"Rest—rest," said Rathbeal soothingly. "Justice shall be done. You are with friends who will not desert you." Returned to Mr. Fox-Cordery. "Have you no word to speak to your victim?"

"I have no knowledge of her," replied Mr. Fox-Cordery. "You are mad, all of you, and are in a league against me."

"You ruined and betrayed her," said Rathbeal, "and then left her to starve. Is it true, Martha?"

"It is true," she moaned. "God have pity upon me, it is true!"

"Liars—liars!" cried Mr. Fox-Cordery. "Liars all!"

"She speaks God's truth, and it shall be made known to man," said Rathbeal.

He did not scruple to search the room for spirits, and he found some in a sideboard.

"Drink," he whispered to her, "and remember that you have met with friends. You shall not be left to starve. We will take care of her, will we not,

Mr. Dixon?"

"I take the charge of her upon myself," said John Dixon. "She shall have the chance of living a respectable life."

"Robert!" said Mrs. Grantham, in a gentle tone. She was standing by his side, holding Clair by the hand. Seeing the woman on the floor she started forward. "Oh, can I do anything? Poor creature! poor creature!"

"We can do all that is required," said John Dixon. "She is getting better already. Go with your husband and child to the inn where we put up the horses. Mr. Grantham knows the way. We will join you there as soon as possible."

Charlotte whispered a few words in his ear.

"Take Charlotte with you, please. She must not sleep another night beneath her brother's roof. Go, my dear."

"Remain here!" cried Mrs. Fox-Cordery, speaking for the first time. "I command you!"

But Charlotte paid no heed to her. Accompanied by her friends, she left her brother's home, never to return.

* * * * * * * *

But little remains to be told. Baffled and defeated, Mr. Fox-Cordery was compelled to sue for mercy, and it was granted to him under certain conditions, in which, be sure, Martha was not forgotten. His accounts were submitted to a searching investigation, and, as John Dixon had anticipated, it was discovered that only a portion of Mrs. Grantham's fortune was lost. Sufficient was left to enable her and her husband and child to live in comfort. Purified by his sufferings, Robert Grantham was the tenderest of husbands and fathers, and he and those dear to him commenced their new life of love and joy, humbly grateful to God for the blessings he had in store for them.

Neither were Little Prue and her mother forgotten. Each of those who are worthy of our esteem contributed something toward a fund which helped them on in the hard battle they were fighting.

A month later our friends were assembled at the wedding of Charlotte and John Dixon. The ceremony over, the newly-married couple bade their friends good-by for a little while. They were to start at once upon their honeymoon.

"It is a comfort," said Rathbeal, shaking John heartily by the hand, "in our travels through life to meet with a man. I have met with two."

"I shall never forget," said John, apart to Mrs. Grantham, "nor will Charlotte, some words of affection you once addressed to her. We know them by heart: 'If the man is true,' you said, 'and the woman is true, they should be to each other a shield of love, a protection against evil, a solace in the hour of sorrow.' Charlotte and I will be to each other a Shield of Love. Thank you for those words, and God bless you and yours."

The last kisses were exchanged.

"God protect you, dear Charlotte," said Mrs. Grantham, pressing the bride to her heart. "A happy life is before you."

"And before you, dear Mrs. Grantham," said Charlotte, hardly able to see for the tears in her eyes.

"Yes, my dear. The clouds have passed away. Come, my child; come, dear Robert!"